FROM THE
NANCY DREW FILES

THE CASE: *Find the burglar who's been preying on prominent members of the River Heights Country Club.*

CONTACT: *Wealthy scatterbrain Joanna Tate, whose weakness for gossip costs her a priceless diamond and ruby necklace.*

SUSPECTS: Zach, *the overfriendly bartender who listens very closely when his patrons chat.*

Cindy, *the cute little redhead who can't seem to keep her hands off other people's property.*

Mike, *the good-looking lifeguard who has a habit of asking personal questions—especially about valuable objects.*

Rita, *the blond masseuse who hears lots of intimate details—including where her clients store their expensive trinkets.*

COMPLICATIONS: *Rookie police detective John Ryan is trying to keep Nancy off the case—to make sure he gets all the credit for cracking the mystery.*

Books in THE NANCY DREW FILES® Series

Available from ARCHWAY paperbacks

THE NANCY DREW FILES™ CASE · 18

CIRCLE OF EVIL

Carolyn Keene

AN ARCHWAY PAPERBACK
Published by POCKET BOOKS • NEW YORK

AN ARCHWAY PAPERBACK *Original*

An Archway Paperback published by
POCKET BOOKS, a division of Simon & Schuster, Inc.
1230 Avenue of the Americas, New York, N.Y. 10020

Copyright © 1987 by Simon & Schuster, Inc.
Cover artwork copyright © 1987 by Gabriel
Produced by Mega-Books of New York, Inc.

ISBN: 0-671-64142-5

First Archway Paperback Printing December 1987

10 9 8 7 6 5 4 3 2 1

NANCY DREW, AN ARCHWAY PAPERBACK and colophon are registered trademarks of Simon & Schuster, Inc.

THE NANCY DREW FILES is a trademark of Simon & Schuster, Inc.

Printed in the U.S.A

IL 7+

Chapter
One

WITH A SMILE, Ned Nickerson leaned toward Nancy Drew and put his lips close to her ear. "I thought this was supposed to be a small party," he said loudly. "So far, I've counted thirty people, and another twelve are just walking in the door."

Laughing, Nancy raised her voice so Ned could hear her over the pounding rock music. "Maybe this is small to Joanna," she shouted. "After all, forty-two people barely fill one wing of this house."

It was true. Joanna Tate's home was such a

huge, sprawling place that people jokingly called it the River Heights Hotel. The Tates were rich, and they loved to spend money —on their house, their cars, jewelry, antiques, and especially travel. That was the funny thing about them, Nancy thought. They had a fantastic house filled with just about everything money could buy, and they hardly spent any time in it. The three of them had barely arrived home from a month-long trip to Europe when Mr. and Mrs. Tate repacked their bags to catch another plane, this time to Mexico. When Joanna had invited Nancy to the party, she said she was tired of being on the move and wanted to spend a few weeks just lounging by the pool of the River Heights Country Club.

The club was where Nancy and Joanna had met. Nancy's father, lawyer Carson Drew, belonged to it, and so did the Tates. As a detective, Nancy was usually too busy working on cases to spend any time there, but one of the few times she had been there she struck up a conversation with Joanna.

Actually, Joanna was the one who had started the conversation. She loved to talk, Nancy discovered, especially about things she had just bought or was about to buy. Nancy had never known anyone more into *things* than Joanna, and if it weren't for her great sense of humor, her conversation would be boring after a while. In fact, the two of them didn't have much in common except that they were both eighteen and they were both girls. But they had become friendly in spite of their lack of common ground, and Joanna had invited Nancy to her next big bash. Nancy had just finished a case and was definitely in the mood for a party.

"This band is great," she said to Ned, looking around the terrace where the five-piece band was playing. It was a warm summer night, and a lot of people had come outside to dance. "I should have known Joanna wouldn't just pop a cassette into a tape deck. Trust her to hire a live band." Tossing her reddish blond hair back from her face, she stood up and took Ned's hand. "Come on, let's dance!"

The two of them found space on the crowded terrace and danced five songs, until the band took a break. Then they went inside and made their way to the refreshment table, where there was enough food to feed a small village for a year. Nancy was trying to decide between a piece of the twelve-foot-long hero or a slice of pepperoni pizza when Bess Marvin and Bess's cousin, George Fayne, Nancy's two best friends, joined her and Ned.

"Isn't this incredible?" Bess shook her long blond hair and laughed as she piled food on

3

her plate. "I guess I'll have to start my diet tomorrow."

George, who was tall and slim and never had to watch her weight, laughed, too. "I keep telling you that you don't need to go on a diet. All you need is more exercise."

"I do exercise," Bess protested. "I just danced for half an hour, thanks to that fabulous band. I never knew what you saw in Joanna," she said to Nancy, "but I have to admit, she does know how to throw a great party."

"Where is Joanna, anyway?" Ned asked. "I haven't seen her since we got here."

"Probably trying on another outfit she bought in Europe," George commented.

"There she is," Nancy said, and they all turned as Joanna Tate, a short girl with frizzy brown hair and a wide smile, burst into the room. As George had said, she was wearing an outfit that couldn't have been bought at a River Heights shopping mall, but her clothes didn't stand out as much as her voice. As usual, Joanna was talking a mile a minute.

"Nancy!" she cried, edging her way over to the food table. "Hi! Glad you all could make it."

"It's great to be here," said Nancy.

"The band is excellent!" Bess exclaimed. "And your dress is gorgeous."

Joanna twirled around so that Nancy, Bess, George, and Ned could get the full benefit of her electric blue silk dress, which was embroidered with hundreds of tiny pearls. When she finished modeling, she asked, "Oh, Nancy, did I tell you about my new necklace yet?"

"Necklace?" Nancy shook her head. "I don't think so."

"Well, actually, I'm not supposed to mention it, but it's so fabulous that I just can't keep it a secret a minute longer!" her voice lowering a bit.

"Why should you have to keep a necklace secret?" George asked.

"Because," Joanna explained, "it's very rare and very valuable. It once belonged to a Russian countess, and my daddy paid a small fortune for it. He promised to give it to me when I'm twenty-one." She rolled her eyes and giggled. "If he knew I was even talking about it, he'd cancel my credit cards!"

"That must be some necklace," Ned remarked.

"It is," Joanna agreed. "It's absolutely gorgeous. I wish you could see it. It's got diamonds and rubies as big as marbles!" Without waiting for anyone to answer, she turned to another group of people and started telling them all about the fabulous necklace her father had brought back from Europe.

Laughing, Nancy and her friends went back to filling their plates with food, but before they had managed to swallow more than a bite or two, Joanna was back. "I just can't stand it!" she said dramatically. "That gorgeous necklace is sitting in the house this very minute, and I just have to show it off or I'll die. I'm going to get it now, but you have to promise me that you'll never breathe a word of this to my parents. Okay?"

"Look, if your parents really don't want you to, maybe you should just forget it," Ned suggested.

"Right," George agreed. "Besides, I don't think anyone's all that interested in seeing it. Most people just want to keep on partying."

"Believe me, they'll forget about everything else once they set their eyes on this necklace," Joanna told them. "I'm just going to sneak it out, give everybody a quick peek, and then sneak it back. Don't go away. I'll only be a few minutes!" Giggling with excitement, she took off through the crowd, telling everyone what she was about to do.

Nancy laughed. "I don't know how she expects to keep her parents from knowing. She's already told everybody about that necklace."

"George was right, though," Bess remarked. "Joanna's the only one who really cares about it. I mean, an old necklace is nice, but I'd rather dance. Besides, at the rate she's moving, by the time she gets upstairs, the party will be over."

"Bess does have a point," Ned said as he watched Joanna make her way through the crowd. He turned to Nancy. "Come on, let's try to find a place to sit. I'm starving."

Carrying two plates of food, Ned started moving through the crowded living room, looking for a chair, a footstool, or even a clear space on the floor. Nancy followed, carrying two glasses of soda.

"I guess we'd better go out to the terrace," Ned called over his shoulder. "I don't see an empty square inch in here."

"Fine," Nancy called back. "I could use the air, anyway."

Together, they stepped through the sliding glass doors that led to the terrace. Just as they did, the band started playing again, and everyone began dancing. The couple closest to the doors whirled around and crashed into Nancy. One of the sodas flew up, splashing her face and hair, and the other fell down, soaking her blue skirt and dripping through her sandal.

"Sorry about that!" the couple called out, dancing away.

Nancy wiped her face with her hand, which immediately became sticky, too. "I was a little hot," she said, joking. "But I wasn't quite ready to take a shower." Glancing down at her skirt, she shook her head. "Well, it doesn't show too much, I guess."

"Sure," Ned said. "That big splotch looks like part of the pattern."

"Thanks a lot," Nancy replied with a laugh. "Yuck! Even my sandal's sticking to my foot. I've got to go wash it off. Be right back."

Pushing her wet hair off her forehead, Nancy threaded her way back through the crowded room, past the food table, and into a hallway. She had never been in the Tates' house before, but she knew a house that size would have plenty of bathrooms. She was right. She found one along the hall and another around a corner. Unfortunately, both of them were occupied.

Nancy kept walking down the hall, then took a right turn, and finally a left. She ended up at the bottom of a short stairway. Nancy climbed the few stairs and found herself in another hallway. She was in a different wing of the house then, she realized. It was quiet; the music from the band and the laughter of the guests sounded far away.

The hall was wide, with a deep, soft carpet and several closed doors on either side. One of them has to be a bathroom, Nancy thought.

Stopping in front of the first door, she raised her hand and was just about to knock when she heard something that made her hand freeze in midair.

It was a scream—a sharp, piercing scream —and it was coming from behind that door.

Chapter

Two

FORGETTING ABOUT KNOCKING, Nancy threw open the door and ran into the room. It was a study, with bookcases on three of the walls and a stone fireplace on the fourth. Next to the fireplace was a painting, which had been swung out from the wall like a cabinet door. Behind it was a wall safe, also open. In front of the safe stood Joanna. She was holding a box, staring at it in horror, as if she had found a snake inside.

"Joanna!" Nancy cried. "What is it? What's wrong?"

"Oh, Nancy!" Joanna's small face crumpled, and tears started rolling down her cheeks. "It's gone! I can't believe it! What am I going to do?"

Quickly crossing the room to Joanna's side, Nancy looked at the box she was holding. It was red leather, padded and lined with white satin. It had obviously contained a piece of jewelry—Nancy could see the imprint in the satin—and that piece of jewelry had obviously been a necklace.

"The diamond and ruby one?" she asked Joanna. "The one you just brought back from Europe?"

Sniffing, Joanna nodded. "The one my father paid a fortune for," she said miserably. "The one he's going to absolutely freak over when he finds out it's been stolen. What am I going to do?" she asked again. "If only I hadn't shot my mouth off about it!"

It was true, Nancy thought. Joanna had blabbed about the necklace to everyone, but it was too late to do anything about that. "What about the safe?" Nancy asked. "How many people at the party did you tell about the safe?"

"I didn't tell anyone about the safe," Joanna said positively. "I suppose somebody could have found it, but no one knows the combination except my parents and me."

"You're sure?" Nancy asked.

"Absolutely."

Stepping closer, Nancy looked carefully at the lock on the safe. It looked perfectly normal, so it couldn't have been broken into, or Joanna would have noticed. Whoever had taken the necklace knew how to pick a lock. Nancy didn't know every person at the party, but she knew most of them, and they were all perfectly regular River Heights teenagers. Not the types who knew about getting into top-quality safes or pulling off a big-time jewelry theft.

"When was the last time you saw the necklace?" she asked.

"Three days ago, when we got home," Joanna said. "I watched my daddy put it in the safe, and I haven't been near it since, until now." Her eyes widened. "You mean it could have been gone all this time and I didn't even know it?"

"Maybe," Nancy said. "Somebody could have gotten into the house, I guess, but I don't think they'd chance it while anyone was here."

"Then they wouldn't have had a problem," Joanna said. "I've hardly spent any time here since we got home, and the maids are both off till my parents get back."

"Listen, Joanna," Nancy said, "I know this

might ruin the party, but we have to call the police."

Joanna sniffed loudly. "I know," she agreed and burst into tears again.

There was a phone on the desk. Nancy crossed to it to dial the River Heights Police Department. After giving her name and the address of the house, she hung up and turned back to Joanna. "They'll be here in about fifteen minutes," she reported.

Wiping her eyes, Joanna grabbed Nancy's arm. "I just got an idea," she said excitedly. "I know the police have to be in on this, but, Nancy, you're a detective, too! And you're good, right?"

"Well, I've been successful before," Nancy said without false modesty. "What's your idea?" she asked, already guessing the answer.

"You try to find the necklace, too," Joanna told her. "I don't care if you work with the police or by yourself. Just help find that necklace before my parents get back. Please, Nancy, I'm really desperate! Will you help me?"

Nancy couldn't help but laugh. "I get it," she said. "If we find the necklace before they get back, then what they don't know won't hurt them, right?"

Joanna nodded.

13

"It sounds nice," Nancy said. "But with the police in on it, I really don't think there's any way to keep it from your parents."

"I guess not." Joanna looked ready to cry again, but after a few seconds, she cheered up. "But if the necklace is already back when they find out about it, it won't be so awful. I mean, how mad can they get if the necklace is safe and sound?"

Nancy laughed again. "I can't argue with that," she said. "Besides, I hate to say no to a new case."

"Oh, Nancy, thank you!" Joanna cried. "I feel better already. I'm just positive you'll solve the whole thing for me!"

"I'll do my best," Nancy promised. "But you've got to help me, too. You've got to tell the police and me everything you know. Don't keep something back just because you're embarrassed about it—like telling an entire party there was a valuable necklace in the house. And don't worry about the police," she went on. "I've worked with them before, and we get along fine. We'll all do everything we can."

Five minutes later, two men from the River Heights Police Department arrived, and Nancy met Detective John Ryan for the first time. He was about twenty-five or thirty years old, and he was handsome, with dark curly hair and blue eyes. He'd be even more handsome if he smiled, Nancy thought. Right now, he looks like he's at the end of a very bad day.

"I thought I knew just about everyone in the department," Nancy said after introducing herself. "You must be new."

"I've been working in Chicago," he said shortly. Looking past Nancy and Joanna, he nodded at the crowded party, which was still going strong. "Nobody's gone home, I hope. We'll have to question everyone."

"Oh, do you really have to?" Joanna asked. "These are all my friends. They wouldn't have stolen the necklace."

"You don't know that for sure," Detective Ryan told her. "Did you tell anyone here about it?"

Blushing, Joanna nodded. "Just about everyone," she admitted.

The detective looked grim. "You'd be surprised what some people will do for money, even so-called friends," he said.

"She didn't tell anyone about the safe, though," Nancy said, trying to be helpful. "All she said was that her father had brought back a necklace. I don't think anyone knew exactly where it was. Besides, whoever got into that safe had to have been a professional. I'm positive that no one that I know here could have done it."

Still not smiling, Detective Ryan gave

Nancy a long look. "Thanks for your opinion, Ms. Drew," he said finally. "Now, if it's all right with you, I'll get on with the official investigation." He told the other police officer to start questioning the party guests, then turned back to Joanna. "I'd like to see the safe now and get a good description of the necklace."

As the three of them walked to the study, Joanna leaned close to Nancy and whispered, "I thought you said you got along great with the police. So why is this guy treating you like you're contagious?"

"I'm not sure," Nancy whispered back. "He doesn't know me, so maybe he thinks I don't know what I'm talking about."

"Well, tell him who you are, then!" Joanna said. "Once he knows, he'll probably be glad to have you on his side."

Nancy turned and sneaked a look at Detective Ryan, who was a couple of steps behind the girls. He was frowning, and his handsome face looked as if it were carved out of stone. "I think I'll wait," she said. "I get the feeling he wouldn't be impressed even if I were Sherlock Holmes."

As Detective Ryan checked out the safe and talked to Joanna, Nancy kept her mouth shut, but she watched him closely and listened carefully. He knew what he was doing, that much was obvious. He asked all the right questions, and he even got Joanna to admit that she might have told a few people about the safe. Not anyone at the party, but maybe some people at the River Heights Country Club, where she had been spending her days.

"Joanna!" Nancy couldn't help butting in. "You didn't tell me about that. You said nobody knew about the safe."

"I guess I forgot." Joanna looked embarrassed. "But I promise, Nancy, that nobody —absolutely nobody—knows the combination." She looked at Detective Ryan. "I've also asked Nancy to help solve this case, and she said she would. She's a detective, too, you know."

As Nancy had predicted, Detective Ryan wasn't impressed. In fact, he looked disgusted. "A detective?" he asked, looking at Nancy.

Nancy nodded.

"An amateur detective, I take it?" Detective Ryan said.

Nancy nodded again. "But I've done pretty well for an amateur," she told him. "And as Joanna said, I promised her I'd help. So, please, let me know what I can do."

When he didn't answer, Nancy continued, saying, "It really doesn't look much like amateur work, does it, Detective? You did take a good look at that safe, didn't you? I think

17

we're dealing with some pretty slick professionals."

Detective Ryan looked coolly at Nancy and raised one eyebrow. "We?" he asked. "What do you mean, 'we'?"

"I told you," Joanna said. "I asked Nancy to help solve this case."

The detective's eyebrow shot up even farther. "If you don't mind, Ms. Tate, I think I'll handle this one my own way. And that means using the police department, not an amateur detective."

"But I do mind!" Joanna protested. "Nancy promised she'd help, and I want her to."

"Sorry, Ms. Tate, but you don't really have any choice in the matter. I'm the detective in charge of the case, and what I say goes."

"Listen, Detective Ryan," Nancy said. "I don't want to butt in, but—"

"Good," he said, interrupting. "Then don't."

Nancy took a deep breath. Detective Ryan was beginning to bug her—a lot. "I was going to say that I guarantee I won't get in your way, if that's what you're worried about. I won't do any harm. And who knows? I just might help."

"What makes you so sure you won't do any harm?" he asked impatiently.

"I guess it's because I know what you have

18

to do to solve a case," Nancy explained. "I've solved some cases on my own, and—"

"That's fine, Ms. Drew," Detective Ryan said quickly. "You just keep on solving your own cases and stay away from mine." He started for the door and then stopped. Turning back, he pointed a finger at Nancy. "I warn you, Ms. Drew. Don't mess with this case."

Chapter

Three

LATE THE NEXT morning, as Nancy turned her blue Mustang into the entrance of the River Heights Country Club, she couldn't help but wonder. There she was, on the case, just twelve hours after Detective Ryan had warned her to stay off it. Should she continue or not?

Detective Ryan didn't know Nancy, of course, so he didn't know that telling her not to follow a case was like telling her not to breathe. But she didn't want to cross him, either. Still, she reasoned, she had promised Joanna she'd help, and she didn't want to let her down. If she was lucky, she could help without the detective even knowing about it, for a while, anyway. She just hoped she wouldn't run into him at the club that day. She wanted a chance to get started on her own before she had to deal with him.

Nancy was usually too busy to spend much time at the club. Despite her schedule, though, she seemed to have been there a lot recently. Before that, she had almost forgotten how peaceful it was, with its emerald-green golf course, its rambling stone clubhouse, and the tiled swimming and diving pools. That day, Nancy intended to follow Joanna and see whom she talked to at the club—and how much she told them about her possessions.

After parking her car in the lot near the clubhouse, Nancy took her green canvas carry-all and walked along the flagstone path that led to the swimming pool. The patio around the pool was crowded with people lounging, tanning, and sipping cool drinks. It seemed as if everyone was talking at once, but the first voice Nancy heard was Joanna's.

"I still can't believe it," Joanna was saying. "I mean, I had to beg my parents to let me stay at home alone, and then this happens! I just don't know what I'm going to do if that necklace doesn't turn up."

Joanna was talking to everyone in general, but the one who was listening the hardest was a tall, good-looking boy with sun-bleached hair and a peeling nose. He has to be a lifeguard, Nancy thought. She had never met a lifeguard who didn't have a peeling nose.

"Nancy!" Joanna called when she saw her. "I'm so glad you're here. I was afraid you might change your mind after the way that detective treated you."

Nancy smiled and shook her head. "Not a chance," she said, easing into one of the lounge chairs.

Sighing in relief, Joanna turned to the lifeguard. "This is Nancy Drew, Mike," she told him. "She's a fabulous detective, and she's going to find out who took my necklace."

"No kidding?" Mike gave Nancy a curious look. "What's your plan for finding it?"

Smiling, Nancy shook her head. "I don't have one yet," she said. Even if I did, she thought, I wouldn't talk about it.

Mike smiled back. He was still staring at her, and Nancy figured he must be a mystery buff. Either that, or he just liked the way she looked in her blue shorts and halter top. "It's kind of funny, though," he remarked, "that you're starting your investigation here at the club. This is nowhere near the scene of the crime, is it?"

"Oh, she just came here to talk to me,"

Joanna chimed in. "She doesn't really have any suspects yet."

"Well, I wish you luck," Mike said, getting ready to climb back up to his lifeguard chair. "Everybody here knew so much about that necklace that we feel like we've been robbed, too."

"Robbed?" a voice said. "Did somebody mention robbery?"

Turning to a woman who had just come out of the clubhouse, Joanna told her all about her missing necklace.

"I know exactly how you feel," the woman said sympathetically. "It was only two weeks ago that our Picasso disappeared. We had just come back from a trip, and we were going to have a party to show off the painting, but it disappeared." She shook her head and sighed. "Most people think we don't have a chance in a million of ever getting it back, either."

"What do the police say?" Nancy asked.

"Not much," the woman told her. "Detective Ryan thinks a professional ring of thieves is behind it and that our painting has changed hands at least five times by now."

So, Nancy thought, Ryan was on that case, too. It would be a nice feather in his cap if he could solve both of them by himself. No wonder he didn't want her help.

In a few minutes, the woman decided to go for a swim. Joanna wanted to get out of the sun for a while, so she and Nancy decided to go into the clubhouse lounge.

On the way, Nancy said to Joanna, "You know, I think it would be better if you didn't tell everyone I'm on the case. It just makes my investigation harder."

"Oh, I'm so sorry, Nancy," Joanna said, putting a hand on her arm. "I didn't think. I'll try to keep my mouth shut from now on. I promise."

"Thanks, Joanna," Nancy said as they entered the lounge. "That will really help."

The clubhouse lounge was a big, bright room with round tables and a long wooden bar on one side. As soon as the bartender saw Joanna, he smiled and waved her over. He was young, with dark curly hair, sparkling black eyes, and a friendly grin.

"That's Zachary," Joanna told Nancy, leading her toward the bar. "He's one of the nicest guys around." She introduced Nancy and ordered lemonade for both of them.

"How's it going, Jo?" Zachary asked, filling their glasses.

"Oh, Zach, it couldn't be worse!" Joanna moaned. "Remember that necklace I told you about?"

"The emerald one that some long-dead princess wore?" he asked.

"Diamonds, rubies, and a countess," Joanna said, correcting. "But it doesn't matter, anyway, because it's gone."

"What do you mean?"

"I mean gone, vanished, stolen!"

Zach gave a low whistle. "Uh-oh. I'll bet your father's really freaked."

"He doesn't know about it yet," Joanna said. "He and Mother are in Mexico."

Zach whistled again, shaking his head. "Boy, you people with money have problems I can't even dream about. You know Mr. Fairchild? Well, he was in here a couple of days ago, telling everybody about some rare book he had just bought. He was going away on a business trip, and he was really proud of the way he'd hidden the book."

"How was that?" Nancy asked.

"Right on the shelf with his ordinary books," Zach said. "He thought it was perfect —no one would think to look for a rare book there. Anyway," he said, going on, "I just hope Mr. Fairchild has a good security system, or he might find himself in the same pickle you are, Jo."

"Nobody could be in the same pickle," Joanna said. "They don't have to face *my* father." Then she brightened up a little. "But at least I have Nancy Drew working for me. She's a detective, Zach, and if anybody can figure out what happened to that necklace, she can."

Zach grinned at Nancy as he poured soda into a glass. "A detective, huh? That's great. I'm crazy about mystery books, read them all the time. What's your theory about the 'mystery of the missing necklace'?"

Before Nancy could answer, the telephone behind the bar buzzed, and Zach answered it. "Sorry," he said after he had hung up. "I have to get some drinks down to the men's locker room. Talk to you later, Jo." Grinning over his shoulder at Nancy, he said, "Good hunting, Detective."

After Zach left, Nancy looked at Joanna and sighed. "Joanna, you just promised me that you weren't going to tell anyone—"

"I know, I know," Joanna said, interrupting. "But Zach's my friend, and I didn't think it would matter if I told him."

"Joanna, it does matter—you could be talking to the thief!"

"Zach?" Joanna asked incredulously. "There's no way." As she took the final sip of her lemonade, she saw Nancy's exasperated expression. "Okay, okay. I won't tell anyone else."

"Please, Joanna. Try."

Joanna signed the check, and the girls headed back to the pool. As they strolled outside, they passed the tennis courts. "Oh, there's Max Fletcher!" Joanna said, waving to a young man who had just finished a game. "Everybody thinks he's the best-looking guy at the club. He's got the most money, that's for sure," she added. "He inherited his father's business—Fletcher Electronics."

Something about that name rang a bell in Nancy's head, but she didn't have time to think about it then. Returning Joanna's wave, Max Fletcher draped a towel around his neck and walked over to the two girls. He was tall and slender, with light brown hair and pale blue eyes. Joanna introduced Nancy to him and then told the story of her missing necklace again—without mentioning Nancy. Max, Nancy noticed, didn't seem too interested.

"Tough luck," he said, opening a new can of tennis balls. "Hey, can I interest either one of you in a game?"

"No thanks," Joanna answered for both of them. "We're a little busy now."

Max sighed. "Too bad. I could use some new competition to keep things exciting." Sighing again, he sauntered slowly back to the courts.

As the two girls continued on in the direction of the pool, Joanna realized that she had left her towel in the lounge. Since it was one of her own towels, they decided to return to the lounge to get it. As they walked, Nancy turned to Joanna. "Just how many people around here did you tell about the necklace, anyway?"

Joanna shrugged. "I don't really know," she admitted. "A lot, I guess. I mean, when you get something new, you just naturally want to tell people about it."

"But, Joanna, you're not talking about a new pair of designer jeans!" Nancy said seriously. That necklace is really expensive!" Of course, she thought, most of the people who belonged to the club also owned really expensive jewelry.

Glancing around the lounge, Nancy saw Mike the lifeguard passing by, probably on a break. He stopped to chat with two men, and Nancy heard him wish one of them a good trip. Zach came back and got into a conversation with a man at the other end of the bar about the man's latest big investment in the stock market. At a nearby table, three women were loudly discussing the trip one of them was about to make and the fact that her house would be closed up for a month.

"Well?" Joanna asked eagerly. "What do you think? Do you have any ideas yet about who did it?"

Nancy didn't answer. She had just realized

something. The lifeguard and the bartender had both known about Joanna's necklace, not to mention Max Fletcher and the dozens of others at the club who had heard her talking about it. People there didn't seem to think twice about telling everyone about the latest rare book or valuable painting they had just bought, where they kept it, and when they were leaving on a trip. Of course, Joanna hadn't been out of town when the necklace was stolen, but she had been at the club every day. And plenty of people knew that.

"I do have some ideas, Joanna," Nancy said finally. "But I can't talk about them yet. First, I've got to pay a visit to Detective Ryan."

"Sorry, Ms. Drew." Detective Ryan shook his head, not looking sorry at all. "I realize you want to help, but I told you before, this is my job. I'll do it."

"But doesn't it make sense?" Nancy asked. "Joanna's necklace and that woman's Picasso were both stolen, and they both spend a lot of time at the club. They—and everybody else there—talk all the time about what they've just bought and where they keep it. And," she said, leaning forward in her chair, "they don't bother to keep it a secret when they're going away and leaving their houses empty. If I were a robber, I'd jump at the chance."

Nancy had hardly been excited about seeing Detective Ryan again, but the more she had thought about the possible country club connection, the more sense it made to her. And even though Detective Ryan didn't want her help, she thought she ought to tell him her theory. As she had driven over to police headquarters, she kept her fingers crossed that he'd be interested. Instead, he was sitting with his blue eyes half-closed, as if he was about to fall asleep.

"Of course," Nancy said, "I still don't have any idea who the robber or robbers are. It could be just about anyone who spends a lot of time at the club—"

"Which really narrows it down, doesn't it?" Detective Ryan said, breaking in sarcastically.

"You know it doesn't," Nancy told him and then she smiled to soften what she had said. "What I'm trying to say is that I think it's worth checking out."

"Ms. Drew, I've got only so many officers," he said with a loud sigh. "Two for this case, to be exact. I've already had one of them out at the club, as a matter of fact, and he came up with zero. The other one's tied up on another case right now. But when somebody gets a free minute, I'll send them back out there. Will that make you happy?"

"I guess it'll have to," Nancy said. "I'm just

trying to help, that's all. I don't understand why you don't want me to."

"This is a matter for the police, that's why." Detective Ryan stood up, his eyes wide open now.

"I know that, Detective Ryan. Except that the police usually appreciate my efforts."

"They do. I've asked around about you. It seems you have a remarkable talent for solving crimes. But this is my case," he said in a tight, angry voice. "And last night, I told you to stay off it, Ms. Drew. I'm saying it again now. And it had better be the last time I have to tell you. Because if it isn't—"

At that moment, his phone rang, and Detective Ryan grabbed it. "What?" he bellowed. His expression changed from anger to surprise and back to anger. He scribbled something on a notepad, said, "I'm on my way," and slammed down the phone.

"Another robbery," he said to Nancy as he strode toward the door. "I suggest you go back to your amateur detecting and let me handle the real thing." Before Nancy had a chance to react to his latest insult, he was gone.

"Oh, what's the use?" she said to the empty office. "It would just make him madder if I told him about my cases, and I don't need that."

Then she noticed that he had left his

notepad behind, and she couldn't resist taking a look at it. When she did, she realized that Detective Ryan could warn her off the case until he was blue in the face, but it wouldn't do any good. On the pad he'd written the name Fairchild. Under that was an address, and under that were the words "rare book."

Victim number three in the country club robberies had just been nailed!

Chapter

Four

I STILL CAN'T believe you're actually going behind that detective's back, Nan," Bess said as she and George climbed into Nancy's car the next day. "I mean, I'm perfectly willing to help, especially since it means spending time at the club, but what if he finds out?"

"I don't know," Nancy said, pulling away from the curb. "Right now, I'm more interested in learning what's going on. I guess I'll just deal with Detective Ryan when and if I have to."

The day before, after she found out about Mr. Fairchild's stolen rare book, Nancy had done a little more snooping around in Detective Ryan's office. She'd discovered that there had been two other robberies besides the ones she knew about. And every one of the victims belonged to the River Heights Country Club.

A few minutes later, Nancy pulled her car into Ned's driveway. Ned gave Nancy a quick kiss after hopping into the front seat with her.

"Oh, Ned, would you mind taking your car? We might need two cars later."

"Okay with me. See you there," he said, pushing down on the door handle. Turning back and leaning into the open window, he asked, "Oh, by the way, what's my assignment, Detective?"

Nancy laughed. "We all have the same assignment," she said. "To listen. Listen for anyone asking questions about other people's vacations. Listen for anyone asking a lot of questions about anyone's new possessions. I don't know if it's a club employee or a member, but I'm convinced there's a connection between that place and the robberies."

"It makes sense to me," George said. "I don't understand why Detective Ryan's being so pigheaded about it."

"Actually, I think he knows there might be a connection, but he just doesn't have enough investigators to do anything about it," Nancy said. Then she laughed. "I guess we're giving him some extra support, whether he likes it or not."

As soon as the four of them arrived at the club, they split up, George heading for the tennis courts, Ned to the men's weight room, and Bess to the golf course. "I don't know a thing about golf, except that it looks extremely boring," Bess commented as she left. "I just hope the caddies are cute!"

After changing into her suit down in the women's locker room, Nancy decided to hang around the pool because she wanted to check out Mike. The day before, when she was there with Joanna, he had watched her carefully. Nancy had figured he was interested in her, but now she wasn't so sure. Maybe he was interested because he knew she was a detective and he was part of the crime. Of course, she was suspicious of just about everyone at this point, and Mike could turn out to be innocent, but she had to start somewhere. And on a warm day, the pool was the perfect place.

Sitting on a lounge chair, Nancy slipped off her sandals. She got up and walked to the edge of the pool. She was wearing a new yellow suit that showed off her long slender legs, and as she stretched her arms above her head, getting ready to dive, she could feel people's eyes on her. She just hoped one pair of those eyes belonged to Mike.

Nancy dived cleanly into the water, surfaced, then began to swim the length of the pool. She was tempted to stay in a long time since it was so cool and refreshing, but after three laps she decided to get out and start her investigation.

Most of the poolside loungers who had watched Nancy dive in didn't pay much attention to her as she climbed out and smoothed her streaming hair back from her face. But glancing casually around, she saw that Mike was watching her.

Good, she thought, pulling a comb through her hair. Let's see what he's really interested in. She sat on one of the chairs and started applying sunscreen. She had just started on her legs when she saw the lifeguard climb down from his chair and head her way.

"Hey," he said when he reached her chair. "Nancy, isn't it? You were here with Joanna Tate yesterday?"

"That's right."

"I thought so. Where's Joanna?" he asked. "She's here almost every day."

"Oh, she said she was too upset to go anywhere," Nancy told him. Actually, Nancy had asked Joanna to stay away from the club for a few days, so she could work without

36

Joanna asking her every ten seconds if she had found the necklace.

Hands on his hips, Mike gave her a big smile. "So? Solved Jo's crime yet?"

"I haven't even started," Nancy told him with a laugh. "If I'd solved it, you can be sure Joanna would have told the whole world by now."

"Yeah, that's true," he said. "Well, do you have any suspects?"

Nancy laughed again, hoping he wouldn't guess that he was one of them. "At this point, your guess is as good as mine. I really haven't spent much time on it."

"Well, I'm sure I don't know as much about solving crimes as you do." Mike grinned and started to go back to his chair. "But I'll bet you won't find your thief here in the swimming pool."

"You're probably right," Nancy said. "But I couldn't resist. Besides, exercise helps me think."

"Okay, I'll let you get to it," Mike told her. "Like I said, I wish you luck."

When he had finally gone, Nancy lay back on the lounge chair, trying to figure out if Mike was just being friendly or whether his friendliness was a cover for trying to learn how much she knew. Sighing, she realized it was much too early to tell about anyone yet.

Nancy stayed by the pool for half an hour more, listening to the conversations around her. Word of the stolen rare book had obviously reached the club, and everyone was talking about it. People were worried about their own houses, but Nancy noticed that the latest robbery didn't keep them from discussing where they hid their own valuable objects. She wanted to tell them all to keep their mouths shut. If Mike or anyone else at poolside was in on the robberies, then the rest of them were sitting ducks.

"Hi there," a voice said nearby. "It's Detective Drew, isn't it?"

Squinting into the sun, Nancy saw that Zach, the bartender, was standing over her, his dark eyes sparkling.

"I'm surprised to see you lying down on the job," he said, joking. "Joanna said you were a great detective, so I figured you'd be out trying to track down the necklace nabber, not soaking up the sun."

Sitting up, Nancy swung her legs over the side of the lounger and laughed. "Promise not to tell Joanna," she said. "If she finds out I've been swimming instead of looking for suspects, she'll never forgive me."

"My lips are sealed," Zach told her. "But just between you and me, do you think maybe the trail starts here at the club?" He shifted the tray of cold drinks he was carrying.

Slowly, without looking at him, Nancy slipped on her sandals. She needed those few seconds to think of what to say and how to say it. Suddenly she remembered what Zach had said about Mr. Fairchild's rare book. And at that moment it hit her—the trail did start there. She was sure of it! Maybe Zach was just asking an innocent question, or maybe he was in on the robberies. It didn't matter at the moment. What mattered was that Nancy suddenly realized that she had to be very careful. If the robbers were there, then they'd know about her interest in the case and would be watching every move she made.

"I'm not sure where the trail starts," she said, casually standing up. "But when I find out, you can bet I'll be on it. Right now, though, I think I'll go into the clubhouse and get something to drink. I've had enough sun for a while."

Smiling at Zach, Nancy made her way slowly into the clubhouse. Max Fletcher was there, she noticed, looking sleepy. When he saw her, he nodded and yawned at the same time, and Nancy wondered how anyone who was head of a big electronics company could be sitting around on a weekday. Then she realized that he probably had plenty of people working for him and didn't always have to go into the office himself.

Nancy ordered a soda, and Zach gave her a big wink as he served it.

What was the wink for? Nancy wondered. Sipping her soda she tried to relax. Forget him for now, she told herself. There are plenty of other people here to keep an eye on.

At that moment, one of those people came into the clubhouse. Mike the lifeguard, probably on a break, walked quickly inside. He looked around, frowned, and then moved off toward a stairway. Nancy took a last sip and decided to follow him. Going down the broad stairway, Nancy found herself in a long, narrow hallway and saw Mike just turning the corner at the end of it. Nancy walked a little faster, passing the women's locker room, and turned at the end of the hall. She passed the boiler room and saw Mike disappear into the men's locker room.

That lets you out, Nancy told herself. But maybe by some lucky coincidence Ned was in there, she thought. After all, that's why he had come—to check out the places she couldn't go.

Nancy doubled back down the hall, and as she passed the women's locker room, she thought that she might as well wash the chlorine out of her hair. She went into the bright yellow- and orange-tiled room, which had at least twenty shower stalls with glass doors.

As Nancy walked in, another girl, who was at the far end of the room, whirled around. She had short, curly carrot-red hair and big brown eyes. She looked frightened.

"Sorry," Nancy said. "Didn't mean to scare you."

"That's okay," the girl said quickly. "I was just leaving, anyway." Dropping a white canvas carryall on a bench, she hurried out of the room.

"Hey, you left your bag!" Nancy called after her. The girl didn't come back, but Nancy decided she probably would once she missed the bag.

Picking up her fluffy white towel, Nancy peeled off her bathing suit and stepped into one of the stalls.

The club is really serious about showers, she thought as she turned on the faucets. Not only was there the usual shower head at the top of the stall, but there was also a second one below it, aiming straight at her stomach, plus a third one on the opposite wall, which would hit her square in the back.

Might as well enjoy it, she told herself, turning the faucets up high. There was a strange clanging sound in the pipes, and in a few seconds the water, which was spraying full force out of all three spouts, turned scalding hot. Nancy reached out for the hot faucet and turned it all the way off, bracing herself for a blast of cold.

But the cold spray never came. The water stayed burning hot, and Nancy plastered herself against the shower door to get out of the direct aim of the spray.

Frantically, she pushed against the shower door, expecting it to pop open. When it didn't, her fright turned to terror. Her skin would start to blister any moment. Giving the door a desperate bang, she cried out, "Help! The door's stuck and I'm getting fried!"

Chapter

Five

TRYING TO AVOID the water, she banged and shouted two more times until, finally, the door was wrenched open by a very surprised-looking woman wearing a large floppy hat and a flowered bathing suit.

Nancy scampered out and wrapped herself in her towel. "Thanks," she said. "I was beginning to turn from rare to medium."

The woman nodded. "It's a good thing I came back for my bag." She peered into the shower, which was still pouring out scalding water. "But I wonder what's happening. These showers were installed just a month ago," she said. As she talked, the woman went over to the canvas bag on the bench and picked it up. Looking inside, she frowned. "Funny. I was sure I put my watch in here."

"That's your bag?" Nancy asked.

"Yes. I have a bad habit of forgetting it," the woman said with a sigh. "And now it looks like I've forgotten my watch, too. I probably left it at home or up by the pool."

Nancy wasn't so sure about that. Remembering the redheaded girl who had dashed out of the locker room so fast, she had the feeling that this woman's watch was long gone. And if that was true, then she had better find out who that girl was. After all, if you're a thief, she thought, why stop with beach bags? Why not go for the big things?

"Oh, listen to me!" the woman said, slapping her forehead. "Here I am, worrying about my watch while you're standing there like a scalded cat! Come with me to the massage room. I'm sure Rita will have something to take the sting away."

Nancy had eased herself into the pair of orange shorts and matching top she'd worn to the club. She followed the woman down the hall. They were just about to go into the massage room when the woman spotted Zach coming around the corner and immediately called out to him. "You won't believe it,

Zach," she said angrily. "Those fancy new showers—one of them just broke and nearly burned this poor girl to a crisp!"

Zach looked at Nancy, worry in his dark eyes. "Are you okay?"

"Oh, sure, I'll be fine," Nancy said. "It felt like I was stuck in there forever, but it was really just a few seconds. The problem was, I couldn't get anything but hot water."

"And the door was jammed, too," the woman reported. "Zach, would you be an angel and call Maintenance to have that door fixed and then call a plumber? I'd do it, but I simply have to get home."

"Oh, that's right," Zach said. "Your daughter's coming for a visit, isn't she? Don't worry, Mrs. Ames, I'll call." He tapped the empty tray he was carrying. "I have to fill another order for the men's locker room, so I'll call from the bar phone." Smiling at both of them, he headed down the hall toward the stairs.

When Zach was out of earshot, Nancy commented to Mrs. Ames, "He seems to know everyone's business around here, doesn't he?"

"Oh, he's just a friendly fellow," was all Mrs. Ames said as she motioned Nancy into the women's massage room. "Now, let's take care of you."

The massage room was small, painted a pale yellow, and had soft music coming out of hidden speakers. On one of the two tables, a woman was stretched out on her stomach, having her shoulders and back kneaded by a small young woman with short blond hair, a friendly round face, and strong-looking hands.

"Rita," Mrs. Ames said, "I've got a casualty for you."

The masseuse turned away from the woman on the table. "What's up, Mrs. Ames?"

When Mrs. Ames explained what had happened to Nancy, Rita went to a white metal closet, pushed aside some jars and gauze, and brought out a small white tube of salve. "This should take care of everything," she said, handing the tube to Nancy. "But if it doesn't, I guess you'd better see a doctor."

"Thanks," Nancy said. "I'm sure it's not that bad."

"You never can tell," Mrs. Ames said with a frown. "Oh, I do hope Zach hasn't forgotten to call the plumber."

"Don't you worry, Mrs. Ames," Rita told her. "You know Zach. When he says he'll do something, it's as good as done."

"That's true," Mrs. Ames agreed, her frown disappearing. "Well, Rita, a massage would be absolutely divine, but I have to rush home and make sure the house is ready." Smiling at Nancy, she left the room and hurried down the hall.

Carefully, Nancy rubbed some salve onto her sore skin. "It feels better already," she reported, sighing as the stinging started to fade.

"Good. I thought it would do the trick." Turning back to the woman on the table, Rita shook her head. "Those new showers are really the pits. Sometimes I think they have minds of their own. I've been scalded twice since they were put in." She laughed. "But at least I was able to get out."

As if she'd suddenly woken up, the woman on the table raised her head an inch. "I've never had a problem," she reported. "And I use them every day."

"Then you've been lucky, Mrs. Davenport," Rita told her. "I can't keep track of all the people who've complained to me about them. Take my word for it," she said to Nancy with a grin, "those new locker rooms cost a pretty penny, but a penny's about all they're worth."

Nancy laughed. "I don't have to take your word for it," she said, smearing lotion onto herself.

"Just be careful next time," Rita advised as Nancy thanked her. "And come on back when your skin's okay. I'll give you a great massage."

Mrs. Davenport lifted her head again. "That I can agree with," she said. Nancy smiled and began to finish up. It was just about time to meet her friends.

Rita turned her attention back to Mrs. Davenport, who had already started to chat. "Now, Rita," she went on, letting her chin drop, "where was I? Oh, yes, that ancient Roman coin. You know, I always thought John's passion for coins was kind of silly. But I must admit, when he bought that one, even I got excited."

"Roman?" Rita asked, digging her strong fingers into Mrs. Davenport's shoulders. "I bet that cost a pretty penny, too."

"Well, I don't really like to talk money, but I will tell you this—it wasn't much under a quarter of a million."

Rita whistled, and Nancy wanted to do the same. Why was Mrs. Davenport telling Rita all this?

"My gosh, I didn't know one coin could be worth that much," Rita said. "If it were mine, I'd be afraid to have it in the house."

"I'm not crazy about the idea, either," Mrs. Davenport said. "But John insists. He says there's no point in having a collector's item if you can't enjoy it."

Nancy was ready to leave, but she waited, holding her breath, to see if Mrs. Davenport would reveal the hiding place of the expensive Roman coin. She wanted to shout at her to keep quiet, but fortunately the phone in the massage room rang, and Rita had to answer it. Nancy and Rita exchanged waves as Nancy left.

Moving slowly down the hall, Nancy realized that she had another suspect—Rita. People weren't any more closemouthed on the massage table than they were at the pool or in the bar, she thought. Of course, Rita could be totally innocent, just like Mike or Zach. She might have asked those questions about the coin just to make conversation.

But she could have another reason for wanting to know how much the coin cost—to see if it was worth stealing. And that remark about being afraid to have something that valuable in the house could have been a hint for Mrs. Davenport to tell her where it was kept.

And there was one more thing, Nancy realized as she climbed the stairs. Mrs. Ames and Mrs. Davenport were both surprised that the shower had broken down. But Rita swore that it happened all the time. Of course, all three of them could be right. But if the showers were fine, then Nancy had either been there the first time they broke down, or else the breakdown had been deliberate. If it was deliberate, she thought, then somebody is trying to scare me off.

Chapter
Six

H ALF AN HOUR later, sitting in a booth at Frank's Pizza with Bess and George, Nancy lifted a slice covered with green peppers and mushrooms and grinned. "This," she said, "is exactly what I need." She took a big bite, leaned back in the booth, and closed her eyes.

"Rough day at the country club?" George asked wryly.

"Don't ask," Nancy said, taking a sip of her soda. "First, tell me what you found out."

"Not much," Bess reported with a sigh. "If I ever have to lift another golf club, I just might hit somebody over the head with it. But the caddies almost made it worth my time," she said and laughed. "They're really cute, every one of them."

"Somehow, I don't think that's what Nancy's interested in," George commented.

"Sure I am," Nancy said jokingly. "Tell me more about the cute caddies, Bess. Did any of them have big ears?"

"I was getting to that," Bess said. "I couldn't tell if they were interested in everything the golfers told them, but they sure got an earful." She swallowed some diet soda and shook her head. "Almost all the golfers talked their heads off about very private stuff—including their possessions—and it was as if the caddies didn't even exist."

"But you said you couldn't tell if any of the caddies were interested?" Nancy asked.

"Not really," Bess said. "See, the people were talking to each other, not to the caddies."

Nancy nodded. "What about you, George? What happened on the courts?"

"A lot of great tennis," George answered with a grin. "The teacher—Jim Matthews—is a former professional, you know."

Nancy nodded. "He's good."

"He's fantastic!" George's brown eyes lit up

with enthusiasm. "There was this guy named Max Fletcher who bet Jim a hundred dollars that he could beat him, but Jim wiped up the court with him."

"I met Max yesterday," Nancy said. "According to Joanna, he wouldn't have any trouble paying up."

"That's for sure," George told her. "He took out a roll of money thicker than his fist and peeled off a hundred-dollar bill. Of course, Jim couldn't take the money. Anyway," she continued, "once Jim saw that I didn't really need lessons, we just played. He won, but I gave him a good game."

"Speaking of money," Bess remarked, "was he interested in anyone's? Max Fletcher's, maybe?"

"No way," George said. "After all, he didn't let Fletcher pay up on the bet. So I'd really be surprised if he were in on the robberies."

"Did anybody tell him about their newest fabulous possession while you were there?" Nancy asked.

"Sure, a couple did," George told her. "But Jim's the quiet type, and when anyone started talking about anything but tennis, he got even quieter, like he was bored."

"That could just be an act," Bess pointed out.

"It could be," George agreed. "But I don't

think it is. I think Jim loves tennis, not money."

"What does Jim look like?" Bess asked.

"Well, he's a little taller than I am," George said. "And he's got brown hair and the most beautiful brown eyes—" Suddenly she blushed. "Okay, I admit it. He's gorgeous."

"And you have a crush on him!" Bess announced. "No wonder you don't think he's up to anything. He could have picked your pocket and you wouldn't have noticed. You were too busy looking at his beautiful brown eyes!"

"Maybe," George admitted, still red in the face. "I still don't think he's in on it, Nancy, but I guess I'm a little prejudiced."

Nancy laughed. "It sounds like we all came up with zero today," she said, reaching for a second slice of pizza. "Wait till you hear what happened to me. I spent three hours at the pool and the clubhouse, and the only things I've got to show for it are a bunch of suspicions and a lot of sore skin."

"Too much sun?" Bess asked.

Nancy laughed again. "Too much water," she said.

Between bites of pizza, Nancy told them all about her hot shower and her encounters with Mike, Zach, Rita, and the redheaded girl.

"Really curly hair?" George asked. "And really red?"

"More orange. Like carrots," Nancy said with a nod.

"I saw her out by the courts," George told her. "And I heard somebody call her Cindy. She kept moving around, hanging out with different people, as though she couldn't make up her mind what to do."

"If you see her again, let me know," Nancy said. "Right now, she's my strongest suspect."

The three of them were still discussing the situation when Ned arrived.

"It's about time," Bess told him. "If you'd been much later, this pizza pan would have been completely empty."

Sliding into the booth beside Nancy, Ned laughed and reached for the next-to-the-last slice. "Sorry I'm late," he said. "But I gave the staff in the weight room a hand setting up a big new machine. Anyway," he said, "I've got news."

"What?" Bess asked hopefully. "Somebody confessed to the whole operation and we can all go home?"

"Not quite," Ned said. "But I think I've got a lead. I was in the locker room—which is a great place, by the way; they even bring drinks down if you phone for them—when a lifeguard came in."

"Mike?" Nancy asked.

"Right. That was his name. He took a shower, and then he was just hanging out, taking it easy, when this other guy came in and started talking to him about some vase he had just bought."

"A vase?"

Ned nodded, swallowing some pizza. "But not just any vase," he said. "It's from some ancient South American civilization or something, and it's worth thousands."

"And Mike was interested?" Nancy asked.

"A lot," Ned said. "I mean, I don't know if he's part of the robberies, but he asked all kinds of questions about it, including where the man kept it. And the man told him—right on the mantel over his fireplace. But that's not the best part." Ned paused to chew his pizza crust.

"Well, don't stop there!" Bess said, complaining. "Drop that crust and tell us what happened!"

"Sorry," Ned said with a laugh. "I'm starving. Anyway, the best part is that the man—Mr. Winslow—told this Mike that he's leaving on a business trip today and that his wife's going with him. He was leaving right then. They're probably driving to the airport now. They'll be gone for a week, he said, and while they're away the house will be empty. How's that for a robber's paradise?"

"It's perfect," Nancy said. "In fact, it's so perfect, I can't resist it."

"What do you mean?" Bess asked.

With a grin, Nancy turned to Ned. "Nickerson, how'd you like to be part of a stakeout?"

"With you?" Ned said. "Anytime, Nancy. Anytime."

At ten o'clock that night, Ned cut the engine on his car and let it coast slowly down the street, stopping it in front of the Winslow house. "The house isn't dark," he whispered, looking up the driveway at the three-story Tudor set back from the street and surrounded by tall trees.

"They probably have the lights on an automatic timer. Are you sure he said the house would be empty? No housekeeper or anyone?" Nancy asked.

"I'm positive," Ned told her. "Mr. Winslow said the housekeeper decided to take her vacation when she learned they were going away. And she's the only other person who lives there."

Nancy and Ned sat and watched the house for a few more minutes while Nancy decided on a plan of action. "Okay," she said softly to Ned. "We're going to have to split up. There's nothing or no one to prevent a burglar from entering at any of the other entrances. I'll find a nice little secluded place on the grounds where I can watch the back door. You stay here. If you see anyone approaching the house—anyone at all—hoot three times like an owl. Then follow them—but not too close."

"Is the hooting absolutely necessary?" Ned asked.

"Do you know how to make any other night sound to warn me? You can't yell, 'Hey, Nancy, intruder approaching on the starboard side.'"

"Okay. Guess you're right," Ned conceded, smiling. "You be careful, though, Detective Drew," he said, leaning over and giving her a quick kiss on the cheek.

Feeling a little like a thief herself, Nancy slipped out of the car and through a gap in the tall hedges that fronted the Winslow property. Once she was on the grounds, it was very dark. The stands of tall trees surrounding the house and grounds shut out some of the moonlight. Everything was in shadow.

As she drew closer to the house, Nancy became increasingly nervous, hoping she wouldn't trip a hidden electronic sensor that would set off an alarm. After each step, she waited, holding her breath and expecting to hear sirens start wailing. But when nothing happened after thirty or forty steps, she relaxed a little and walked more quickly.

Trying not to step on any twigs, Nancy moved cautiously around the house and walked as quietly as possible toward the back. About thirty feet from a back corner was a willow tree, its drooping branches swaying gently in the night air. It was a perfect place to wait, Nancy thought. The branches would hide her, but she could peer out and have a full view of the back and side of the house.

Once hidden by the low-hanging branches, Nancy relaxed a little and checked her watch. Ten-thirty. She just hoped the robbers would decide to show up that night. If they didn't, she and Ned would be up all night every night for the next week. Which would mean they'd have to rely on George and Bess to investigate the club during the day while they slept.

An hour later, Nancy realized that her left foot had fallen asleep. As quietly as possible, she stood up and shook her ankle, trying to get the circulation moving. The stinging, prickly sensation had just started to creep through her foot when she had to freeze, standing on one leg like a stork in sneakers.

A shadow was thrown up against the rear wall of the house. She could see the dark shape of a person slipping swiftly and silently toward the back door.

Chapter

Seven

THIS IS IT! Nancy thought. The stakeout is paying off. The shadow was still there, sliding along the back wall. Her heart thudding, Nancy peered through the branches, hoping to catch a glimpse of the intruder.

As she watched, straining to see, the shadow suddenly began moving very erratically. It was looking for something—the entrance, maybe?

Wanting to see the thief, Nancy pushed a branch aside and poked her head out.

At the sound of the branches being disturbed, the shadow froze. For a few seconds, it remained motionless as though it were a piece of black paper pinned against the stucco and beams. Then, suddenly, it became smaller until it disappeared, and at the same time Nancy heard the sound of feet pounding across what must have been a stone patio. In a moment, the sound changed to a dull thudding as the person hit grass and kept on running.

Without hesitating, Nancy shoved the tangled willow branches apart and took off after her shadowy visitor.

Her foot still had very little feeling. Unable to control it, Nancy stumbled, scraping her knees and the palms of her hands on the rough stones of the patio. But she was up in a second, plunging into the darkness at the rear of the property. A feathery cloud had slid over the moon, making the night pitch-dark.

It was easy going at first, just a gentle sloping hill covered with thick mown grass. But after a couple of minutes, the grass ended, and Nancy found herself in a forest. Low-hanging branches caught at her hair and scratched her face, while dead wood and wet and slippery masses of leaves slowed her until she was almost taking baby steps.

When Nancy stopped to untangle her hair from a vine, she could hear the "shadow" ahead of her, crashing through the woods, not bothering now to be quiet. It wasn't moving quickly either, and Nancy thought she might have a chance to catch up with it. She was just about to plunge ahead, when she suddenly realized she couldn't hear the intruder anymore. Had he finally made his way through the forest? Or was he hiding somewhere ahead, lying in wait for her?

Deciding what to do in an instant, Nancy moved off again as quickly as possible, her arms stretched out in front of her. She expected someone to reach out and grab her at any second. But no one did, and after two or three minutes, she was abruptly stopped by a six-foot-high stone wall. So that's why the mysterious intruder had suddenly stopped making noise—the suspect had climbed the wall and slipped away, probably for good.

Nancy knew it was probably a lost cause by then, but she decided to continue. Maybe the person had fallen and she'd get lucky and find him lying on the ground. Besides, she had gone too far to quit then.

The trees hadn't thinned out, so Nancy easily climbed a maple tree and then stepped from it out onto the wall. The cloud drifted off the moon, and Nancy found herself looking out at a smooth lawn that stretched as far as she could see. Every once in a while, it dipped into a low valley or climbed a small hill, and there were a few clumps of trees here and there. It must be part of somebody's estate, she thought. But it's the biggest backyard I've ever seen.

Forget it, she told herself. The intruder could be anywhere out there. Your chances of finding him are about one in a million. She was just about ready to turn back when something caught her eye. Off to her right, something was moving. She was much too far away to tell what it was, but it didn't matter. If there was movement, Nancy wanted to find out who or what was making it.

Leaping lightly to the grass, she started running again, toward the spot where she had seen the stirring. After the dead leaves and branches of the forest floor, the grass felt like velvet underfoot. In only a couple of minutes, she found herself looking down a grassy slope at a small pond, and beyond that, far off, she could see lights.

Circling the pond, Nancy kept up her pace, all the time wondering whose property she was on. She focused her attention on the distant lights—which looked too bright to be from an individual house—so she didn't see the rock that suddenly tripped her. Falling, she threw out her arms, only to have her hands sink up to the wrists in sand.

A sandbox, Nancy thought, brushing herself off. But as she stood up, she realized that it wasn't a box. It was just a kidney-shaped bed of sand at the bottom of another small, grass-covered hill. And suddenly it hit her—she had fallen into a sandtrap. She wasn't standing in anyone's yard—she was on the golf course of the River Heights Country Club.

Like a shot, Nancy was off again, moving toward the lights, which she knew were the floodlights around the clubhouse. The shadow maker must have headed this way, too, she thought. And she wondered if he'd come from there in the first place. If he had, then that night's gamble had really paid off.

As Nancy drew closer to the clubhouse, she slowed down and strained her ears. Except for the gentle ripple of water in the pools, the complex seemed quiet. She edged her way to a set of sliding glass doors that led into the lounge and tested them.

They were locked. It was late—after midnight—there must not have been any dinner parties or meetings scheduled, and nobody was inside. But someone *is* here, Nancy thought.

Feeling certain that the mysterious shadow maker was close by, Nancy walked cautiously around the clubhouse, testing all the doors. Locked! But that didn't mean the intruder had gone. He might have a key. He could be in the clubhouse right then, watching and waiting to see what she'd do.

But what should she do? She hated to go back. But if she didn't show up at Ned's car soon, he'd come looking for her. And then he'd have the police out looking for her. And with her luck, it would be Detective Ryan.

Frustrated, Nancy turned from the clubhouse and started back, crossing the red tiles that surrounded the swimming area. That was when she saw them—several sets of footprints.

Her frustration disappearing, Nancy moved closer and bent down to examine them. A few pieces of grass and leaves were stuck to the tiles in the shape of footprints. They were facing the club, which meant the owner of them had probably came from the same direction she had.

Straightening up, Nancy followed the prints, which led her beside the swimming pool and over to the side of the square, twenty-foot-deep diving pool. It was dark there, the deep water was inky black, and the two-tiered diving platform looked like a visitor from a distant world.

Wishing she had a flashlight so she could see more clearly, Nancy took a couple of steps. Then she listened and stopped. Silly me, she thought. Just some leaves rustling.

Abruptly, there was a slapping sound on the tiles, and before Nancy could turn, she felt herself being shoved, hard, from behind. Her arms flailing wildly, Nancy fell, the cold, dark water of the diving pool meeting her with a slap.

Before she could orient herself, she felt herself being forced down into the watery darkness. One arm was viciously wrapped around her neck, and the other held her head just below the surface!

Chapter

Eight

DESPERATELY, NANCY PULLED at the arm around her neck, finally sinking all ten fingernails into it. She would have given anything to know the identity of her partner in this lethal underwater ballet. But knowing wouldn't help her breathe. What she needed was air!

Squirming and thrashing, Nancy fought to free herself from the viselike arm around her neck, but nothing seemed to do any good. Suddenly, inspiration struck, and Nancy kicked, thrusting her legs deeper into the water. If she was going to drown, then her assailant would go down with her. Madly, she fluttered her legs, dragging them both toward the bottom.

The lack of oxygen was making her dizzy —her lungs were on fire, ready to burst. At what point her attacker had loosened his grip on her throat, she didn't know, but when the realization struck, she fought to pull herself through the water until her head broke the surface.

For a few seconds, Nancy bobbed in the middle of the pool, gulping in huge lungfuls of air. Then she forced herself to look around —her attacker had fled. She paddled over to the side, where she hung on and rested until her head started to clear and she got her breath back.

Then Nancy scanned the pool area more closely. It was definitely empty. Except for a second trail of footprints—bare, wet ones this time—everything looked exactly the same. Whoever had shoved her into the water was gone.

Nancy slowly dragged herself out of the pool. Sitting on the tiles, she pulled off her sneakers. She was too exhausted to pursue her attacker. Even if, by some miracle, she did catch up to him, she would only collapse at his feet.

Her head was pounding, and the last thing

she felt like doing was thinking. But she couldn't help wondering why her attacker had left the diving pool so suddenly.

Maybe, Nancy thought, he hadn't really wanted to drown her. Maybe he'd just wanted to scare her.

"Hey!"

Nancy jumped as a light blinded her eyes and an angry, harsh voice boomed out of the darkness.

"What are you doing here?" the voice demanded. "This is private property. Boy, I've had it up to here with you kids sneaking into the club, using the pool, trampling the golf course!"

And I've had it up to here with this whole night, Nancy thought tiredly. "Wait a minute," she said. "How do you know I'm not supposed to be here? I'm a member of this club, and so is my father."

"Yeah? Well, you ought to know the rules then," the voice said. "The rules say no one's allowed on the grounds after hours without a pass. Where's your pass?"

Good question, Nancy thought. "I forgot it," she said. "And you haven't told me who you are yet. What gives you the right to treat me like a criminal?"

Slowly, the light bobbed and came nearer.

As it did, Nancy was able to see who was behind it. A very short, very skinny man who didn't look like his powerful voice sounded.

"I'm the night watchman," the man informed her. "Your father—if he really does belong to the club—helps pay my salary. So I have the right to chase you off this property because it's my job."

Nancy suddenly sat up straighter. "When did you go on duty?" she asked.

"Ten, twenty minutes ago."

"Did you see anyone else?" Nancy asked. "Going in or out of the clubhouse, maybe?"

"Nope. I park at the front entrance, walk around the golf course, then cut over to the clubhouse. The place is locked up tight, just like it should be," he said. "I did think I saw someone jogging down the drive. Could have been one of the staff, but since he was on his way out, I didn't stop to check. Besides, I was clear over by the fifth hole."

"He?" Suddenly, Nancy didn't feel tired anymore. "What did he look like?"

"I told you, I decided not to check," the man repeated impatiently. "He was probably part of the staff, like I said. The staff can use this place anytime they want, and they don't need passes. You wouldn't believe how many kids like you decide to have midnight picnics and then leave their trash all over the grass."

"I told you I didn't—" Nancy stopped herself. Arguing wasn't going to do her any good, and if she told the truth, he'd probably call the police. "Look," she said. "You're right. Some friends of mine dared me to sneak in here and go for a swim."

The light swept around as the man observed her soaking clothes and drenched sneakers. "Shoes and all, huh?" he asked skeptically.

"Right," Nancy said, quickly. "After all, if I don't come back wet, they'll never believe I did it."

The night watchman shook his head, obviously disgusted with what he thought was a dumb prank. Then he surprised Nancy by giving a short laugh. "Maybe that guy I saw leaving wasn't staff after all," he said, laughing again. "Maybe it was one of your friends, checking up on you."

Some friend, Nancy thought. "Listen," she said, standing and picking up her shoes. "I've never done anything like this before, and, believe me, I don't plan on doing anything like it again. Why don't I just get out of here now, and we'll both forget the whole thing?"

"I'm not about to forget it," the man told her. "But I think your getting out of here sounds like the best idea you've had all night."

"You're right about that," Nancy said, and she started off toward the golf course.

"The entrance is that way," the man said, waving his flashlight in another direction.

"But I have to pretend I'm sneaking back out," Nancy called. "It's all part of the dare."

Shaking his head again, the man finally let her go. Nancy skirted the pool and the lounge chairs, moving quickly until she reached the golf course and was out of his sight.

So, she thought, as she headed barefoot toward the pond, the people who work here can come and go as they please. The night watchman must know them all, so if he sees any of them here at night, he wouldn't be the least bit suspicious. That's very nice. And if some of the people who work here just happen to be using it as a base of operations for a bunch of robberies, then that's also very nice —for them.

It could be someone on the staff, Nancy thought. But who? And what about Rita or Cindy? Just because it was a man who had attacked her in the pool didn't mean one of the women wasn't involved. She could be working with someone. Or a few people could all be working together.

How many people were involved, and who they were, Nancy didn't know yet. But she did know one thing—they were on to her. That night had definitely been a warning.

Well, Nancy thought, there's no way I'm

going to back off. I'm just going to have to be more careful, that's all. And she had to warn Bess and George and Ned, too.

Thinking of Ned, Nancy began to hurry. She'd been gone a long time—he must be going crazy, wondering what had happened. Once she reached the wall at the edge of the golf course, she forced her feet into the sopping sneakers, found a low point in the wall that had crumbled a bit, and climbed over.

The woods weren't any easier to get through on the way back, and by the time Nancy reached the edge of the Winslow property, she felt completely drained. A shower, she thought. A hot shower, then some dry clothes, and then food. A cheeseburger and a chocolate shake. And fries. Lots of fries.

Her stomach rumbling, Nancy passed the willow tree she had hidden beneath, hurried by the house and through the trees in the front, and finally stepped through the hedge and onto the street. Then she stopped, her mouth falling open in amazement.

Ned was still there. But instead of sitting in his car, he was leaning against it, his face turned sideways and pressed up against the roof as Detective John Ryan frisked him.

Chapter

Nine

"Hey!" Nancy couldn't believe what she was seeing. "What's going on?" she shouted, running the last few yards to Ned's car.

Detective Ryan barely glanced at her. "What's going on is the apprehension of a suspicious character," he said. "Not that it's any of your business, Ms. Drew."

"Suspicious?" Nancy almost laughed. "Believe me, Detective, there's absolutely no reason to suspect Ned of anything."

"I suppose you know him?"

"Yes, I do. He's my boyfriend, Ned Nickerson."

74

"And I suppose you're going to tell me that he has a good reason for prowling around one of the wealthiest neighborhoods in town?" Detective Ryan continued searching Ned.

"I already told you the reason," Ned said, still leaning against the car. "I was looking for my date."

"That's right," Nancy said. "And here I am, so now you have to believe him."

The detective finally let go of Ned and turned to face Nancy. When he saw her wet hair and clothes, and the scratches on her face and hands, he frowned. "Is this the latest way to dress for a date?" he asked sarcastically.

"Of course not," Nancy said, trying to think of a way to explain things. "We were driving around, and—I thought I saw somebody sneaking around this house. So I got out of the car to look around, and Ned waited for me."

"Right," Ned said. "When she didn't come back, I went looking for her. I walked around the house, and then I drove around the neighborhood a few times. Then I decided to come back to the house one last time and look around. That's why whoever called you said I was prowling."

"Called?" Nancy asked. "You got a call about Ned?"

The detective nodded. "An anonymous tip.

Somebody reported a prowler on the grounds of the Winslow house."

"When was this?" Nancy wanted to know.

"Fifteen minutes ago."

Fifteen minutes, Nancy thought. Just enough time for my pool companion to get to a phone to call the police. He would have guessed I had to come back here.

"But I think I've answered enough questions," the detective said, breaking into her thoughts. "What about you, Ms. Drew? Do you always hop out of cars every time you see someone walking around a house?"

"No, I don't," Nancy said, knowing he wasn't going to like what she had to say. "But I knew the Winslows were leaving town, and I knew their house would be empty. They probably have a lot of valuable stuff in there, so I—"

"So you just decided to take things into your own hands," the detective said interrupting. "Look, Ms. Drew, I warned you before, and I'm going to warn you just one more time —stay off this case."

Without waiting for an answer, the detective opened the door of Ned's car and motioned Nancy to get inside. Ned slid in next to her and started the engine. Before he could pull away, though, Detective Ryan leaned down to the passenger window, a frosty look in his blue eyes. "Just one more thing, Ms. Drew. You never did explain why you're soaking wet. What did you do, fall into the Winslows' pool?"

"Well, it was awfully warm, Detective," Nancy answered. "And the water was very cool. Let's just say I couldn't resist it."

As Ned drove away, Nancy leaned back against the seat and closed her eyes. "I wanted to tell him everything that happened tonight, but I got the feeling he wouldn't have listened to a word I said."

"What *did* happen, anyway?" Ned asked.

"I did go for a swim," Nancy said. "But as I told Detective Ryan, I just couldn't resist."

While Ned drove through the quiet streets, Nancy told him what had happened after she left him.

"Joanna let the whole world know who I was, so that made me a very easy target," she said, finishing her story as Ned pulled up in front of the Drews' home. "But at least I'm sure I'm on the right trail. Whoever's behind those robberies has to have something to do with the country club. That's certain now."

"Right." Ned agreed and slipped an arm around her shoulders, pulling her close. "The question is who? And what are we going to do now?"

Nancy leaned back against him, relaxing for

77

the first time that night. "Keep looking," she said.

"But as you said, they're probably on to you. And that dunking tonight wasn't just for fun," Ned commented. "They're dangerous, and you've been warned to back off."

"I know," Nancy said. "I'll just have to keep my eyes open wide from now on. And so will Bess and George and you," she said, turning to kiss his cheek. "At least they haven't seen any of us together at the club. But we'll have to be careful to keep it that way."

After kissing him again, Nancy got out of the car and walked up to her house, her squishy sneakers leaving wet prints on the front walk. She remembered the prints she had seen earlier, and she knew she had to find out who had made them before he followed her again.

The next day, Nancy arrived at the club alone. Because George and Bess weren't members, Nancy had given them passes and told them to come individually, too. Ned was to stay away that day.

First, Nancy walked down to the tennis courts, hoping that maybe Cindy had decided to hang out there. She saw George and Jim playing a game, and she saw Max Fletcher. But there was no one around with flaming red hair, so she headed for the pool.

It was hot. The pool was packed, and Mike, as head lifeguard, was on duty as usual. He was too busy keeping an eye on the crowds to listen to conversations about people's valuables, or even to take a break. Nancy watched him for a few minutes, wondering if he was as good at drowning people as he was at saving them. He was big enough to have held her under water the night before.

Soon she went into the lounge, which was more crowded than the pool. Zach was working, as were two other bartender-waiters. They were scurrying around, filling glasses with soda, iced tea, and lemonade. Even Zach, who was usually so chatty, didn't stop at a single table for more than five seconds. He did find time to throw Nancy a quick wink; except for that, though, he was on the run.

Nancy had hoped to speak to everyone working in the lounge. If she was careful about the questions she asked, she might have learned something. But unless the crowds suddenly thinned out, she wouldn't get the chance.

There's still Rita, she thought. Even though it had been a man in the pool with her, that didn't mean Rita wasn't in on the robberies in some way. After all, she got an earful while she gave her massages.

When Nancy got downstairs, Rita was busy. Nancy wanted to wait and eavesdrop but decided that might be a little too obvious. Instead, she just asked if Rita had an opening, then walked down the hall to the women's locker room, where she locked up her bag. Might as well get some exercise while I'm waiting, she thought, and she went into the weight room.

Half an hour later, Rita stuck her head around the weight room door and told Nancy she could take her then. Her arms and thighs feeling like dead weight themselves, Nancy followed Rita into the massage room.

"Hop on the table," Rita said with a smile. "I'll loosen you up."

Within fifteen minutes, the soreness had left Nancy's muscles, and she felt so relaxed she wanted to take a nap. Rita knew her business, she thought.

"You look like you're falling asleep," Rita remarked, pounding Nancy's legs with the sides of her hands. "Want me to call up to the lounge and order you a drink?"

"I think they're too busy up there," Nancy said. "The place is jumping."

"Oh, right," Rita said. "Well, I've got a quick call to make, if you don't mind. It'll just take a second." While Nancy waited, her eyes closed, Rita spoke into the phone. "Just wanted to let you know that I can't make it," she said. "But I'll be in touch, okay? 'Bye."

Turning back to Nancy, Rita sighed. "Boy, am I glad to be inside on a day like this! I don't see how anybody can stay out in the sun when it's so hot. Of course, it's mostly the kids who do. The older people all come inside and sit around talking."

"Everybody's very friendly at the club," Nancy said.

"That's for sure." Rita laughed. "I can't believe some of the things people tell me. They talk about their love lives and their problems, their jobs—"

"And their money." Nancy finished for her. "The older people around here talk a lot about that, don't they?"

Laughing, Rita dug her fingers into the back of Nancy's neck. "Well, most of them have plenty of it, so I guess it's normal to talk about it."

"I suppose," Nancy said. "But I think if I were really rich I'd be more discreet about it."

Rita laughed again. "I would, too. If I had what some of them have, you can bet I wouldn't tell a single living soul."

But does she have what they have? Nancy wondered. Or some of what they have, like an antique necklace and a painting by Picasso? And if she does, how am I going to find out? Rita talks, but she doesn't really say much.

Five minutes later, Nancy decided to give up on Rita, for the moment, anyway. Yawning, she walked to the locker room. Just before she turned in the door, she saw a short, slender girl with hair the color of carrots come out of the weight room. It was Cindy.

For a second, Cindy stood completely still, her large eyes wide and staring. Then, suddenly, she leaped forward, brushed past Nancy, and raced for the stairs, taking them two at a time.

Nancy raced after her, up the stairs and into the crowded lounge. She glanced around, certain she could spot that hair anyplace, but there was no sign of it. Cindy couldn't be that far ahead, she thought, and she made her way as quickly as possible through the crowd and out into the pool area.

The patio was packed. Nancy looked everywhere, but there was still no sign of Cindy. Skirting the pool area, she was just about to head for the tennis courts when she heard the squeal of a car's tires.

Turning, Nancy was just in time to see a small yellow convertible peel out of the parking lot and head down the entrance drive. She was too far away to spot the license number, but there was no question about who the driver was. Cindy's hair looked as if it were on fire.

Frustrated, Nancy watched the car disappear down the drive. Cindy was feeling very guilty, that was obvious. But about what? Rifling through Mrs. Ames's beach bag? Or stealing from people's houses? Or both?

Still thinking about it, Nancy went back into the clubhouse and down to the locker room.

After she opened her locker, Nancy pulled out her canvas bag and was going to sling it over her shoulder. But then she noticed a white envelope sticking halfway out of the side pocket. Curious, she took it out and opened it. Inside was a piece of paper with a typed message. The message read: "We know what you're up to. But does your father? Forget about finding us, or we'll arrange a meeting with him—by the diving pool. How long can he hold his breath?"

Chapter

Ten

I UNDERSTAND WHY you're worried, Nancy," Carson Drew said after she had called him at his law office and explained what had happened. "But I'm leaving for New York tonight, remember? I'm going straight from the office. Actually, I have to leave in ten minutes or I'll miss the plane." He laughed lightly. "I think I'll be safe between here and the airport."

"I'm not worried about right now, Dad," Nancy said. She knew her father was leaving town—he was going to visit some friends and attend a lawyers' meeting in New York for a day or two. So she had rushed straight home from the club to warn him before he went. "I'm worried about when you come back. After all, you'll be home soon, and these people are serious."

"It certainly sounds like it," her father said. "Which is why I'm more worried about you than about me. Don't you think you should go to the police on this one?"

"I want to give it a little more time," Nancy said with a sigh. "I told you about Detective Ryan, remember?"

"I take it you two still haven't hit it off."

"No. He thinks I'm a giant pain in the neck." Nancy shook her head. "Anyway, I'm being careful. Don't worry."

"Well, I'm sure you think you know what you're doing, but just remember, you don't have eyes in the back of your head," her father said, warning her. "Forget about me, and look out for yourself."

Nancy agreed, but she knew she wouldn't be able to stop worrying. To have her father threatened was frightening. She was glad he was going to be out of town, but she couldn't stop thinking about what might happen when he came back.

As Nancy was pacing restlessly around the kitchen, going over everything she had discovered so far and not coming up with anything new, Hannah Gruen, the Drews' housekeeper, came in.

"You look like a cat stalking a bird," Hannah remarked.

Nancy laughed. Hannah had been with the Drews for fifteen years, and she knew Nancy's moods better than anyone. "I *am* stalking a bird," Nancy said. "More than one, I think. The problem is, I can't decide which one to go after."

"It's this new case, isn't it?" Hannah asked.

Nancy nodded, deciding not to mention the threat to her father. There was no sense in having Hannah lose sleep over it, too. Not yet, anyway. "I'm on the right track," she said. "But I don't have any concrete theories or clues. It's beginning to get pretty frustrating."

"Well, do you think wearing a path in the kitchen floor will help?" Hannah asked. Nancy glanced down sheepishly. "Why don't you play some music or do something to relax?"

"I guess I'll have to," Nancy said. Then she realized that she was still wearing the same sweaty shorts and shirt she had worked out in, and her hair was tangled and matted. "But first, I think I'll shower and change. It might not help me solve the case, but at least I'll feel human again."

"By the way," Hannah said as Nancy started to leave, "I'm going to a meeting at the library in a little while, so I won't be here for dinner. And since your father won't be here, either, it's leftovers for you."

"Fine," Nancy said, knowing she wouldn't be hungry, anyway. "I'll see you when you get back."

After a shower, Nancy dried her hair, put on a flowered cotton skirt and a white tank top, and pushed a rock tape into her tape deck. Bess and George might be home by then, she decided, and she wanted to find out if they had learned anything.

"Absolutely nothing," Bess reported when Nancy called. "It was exactly the same as yesterday, except there weren't as many golfers because it was so hot. The only difference was that one of the caddies was even more friendly to me than he had been yesterday." Bess giggled. "I was pretty friendly to him, too, which wasn't hard because he is *so* gorgeous!"

"Did you find out where any of them were last night?"

"Three of them talked about nothing but last night's baseball game, and they said they watched it at one of their houses," Bess said. "Of course, I suppose they could have been lying, but they discussed every hit and strike as though they'd been sitting in the stands."

"What about the other two?" Nancy asked.

"One said he was sick, and, believe me, he was croaking like a frog," Bess told her. "And Tom—he's the gorgeous one—well, he and I were talking on the phone for almost an hour. And that was at the time you were out getting soaked."

Nancy felt relieved. If Bess was right, then there were five people she didn't have to follow. "Okay, thanks," she said. "I'm going to call George now and see if she's got any leads."

"George has a date," Bess told her. "With her handsome tennis teacher. But she told me to tell you that he didn't act any differently today, either. She didn't find out what he was up to last night, but she's going to try to find out tonight."

"Good." For George's sake, Nancy hoped that the tennis instructor had a perfect alibi.

After she hung up, Nancy felt hungry and looked for something to eat. She found half a roast chicken and salad makings in the refrigerator, but it wasn't what she wanted. Remembering the cheeseburger and fries she hadn't eaten the night before, she called Ned and suggested they go out. Half an hour later, the two of them were sitting in a booth at the Burger Barn.

Nancy bit into a crisp fry and smiled. "If I

didn't have this case on my back, I'd be perfectly happy right now."

"Nothing new to report?" Ned asked.

"A little," Nancy said, telling him about her chase after Cindy. "I'd really like to talk to that girl. She's the only one I've seen who even acts suspiciously. She could have put the note in my locker. But that doesn't mean there aren't others in on it, too. Oh, Ned, I don't know. I really can't rule anyone out yet."

Ned smiled. "So what's your next step, Detective?"

"I guess I'm going to have to put their names into a hat, pick one, and follow that person after he or she leaves the club." Nancy laughed. "Maybe I'll get lucky."

"I don't think another stakeout would work, not at the Winslows' anyway," Ned said. "I have a feeling Detective Ryan has that covered. And I'm not so sure following these people is such a good idea."

"But I don't know what else to do," Nancy said, arguing. "I can't keep hanging out at the club—watching. They don't even do their dirty work there."

"They do part of it there," Ned reminded her. "They get all their information at the club. Plus, I just thought of something. The club would make a great place to hide stuff. It's got hundreds of lockers. And who knows? One of them might be filled with stolen goods instead of soggy towels."

"I didn't think of that." Nancy swallowed the last bite of her cheeseburger and grinned. "Did you ever consider becoming a detective?"

"Why bother?" Ned said with a laugh. "I've got you, remember?"

As Ned drove Nancy home, the two of them joked and laughed and talked about everything but the case. It felt good, Nancy thought, to forget about it for a little while. She decided to try not to think about it the whole night. Maybe all the clues would fall into place in the morning.

"Did I tell you how great you look tonight?" Ned asked as they got out of the car and walked to Nancy's house.

Nancy shook her head, smiling. "If you did, I didn't hear it. Go ahead, tell me again."

"You do look great," Ned said softly, reaching out and pulling her closer.

They were on the front porch then, and just as Ned was about to kiss her, Nancy pulled away, staring over his shoulder.

"What is it?" Ned asked.

"The door," Nancy said, pointing. "It's

partly open. And I remember locking it when I left."

"Maybe Hannah's home," Ned suggested, "and she just didn't shut it all the way."

Checking her watch, Nancy shook her head. "It's too early. And, anyway, if she were home, she'd have turned on the porch light."

Slowly, Nancy pushed the door open and stepped inside. She was sure Hannah wasn't there, but just in case, she called her name, three times. There was no answer.

Behind her, Ned said quietly, "I'll check the kitchen." Nancy heard his footsteps as he cautiously made his way into that room. She continued walking slowly through the house, peering into one room after the other. They were all empty, and nothing even looked disturbed.

Maybe I just didn't pull the front door closed tightly enough, she thought, trying to remember. It had never happened before, but there was always a first time.

Nancy was just starting to relax when she reached her father's room. One look, and her heart started pounding again. The door was closed. Carson Drew never shut it except when he was changing his clothes.

Her mouth dry, Nancy quietly put her hand on the doorknob, counted to three, and threw the door wide open.

A curtain billowed as the door opened, but nothing else moved. Slowly scanning the room, Nancy saw that the bed was made, the closet door was closed, the drawers were shut. Then her eyes moved up to the ceiling. There, dangling from the light fixture, was one of her father's neckties—made into a noose! Attached to it was a note scrawled in greasy bloodred lipstick:

Your dad might be gone now, but he has to return sometime. We'll be waiting. Get off the case, Nancy Drew!

Chapter

Eleven

STARING AT THE ugly message, Ned whistled softly. "Don't you think it's about time to call the police, Nancy?"

Nancy shook her head. "If it was anybody but Detective Ryan, I'd say yes. But he'd tell me it was all my own fault for messing around in police business."

"But if you tell him why it happened —because you're getting too close to the robbers—then he'd have to listen," Ned said.

"Maybe," she said. "But if he brings the police in and lets them swarm all over the country club, I guarantee there won't be another robbery in River Heights—at least not by these people. I haven't scared them off because they know I'm working alone and they think they can scare *me* off. But they wouldn't bother to threaten a whole police force. They'd just lie low until the whole thing blew over.

"Let's get this picked up before Hannah comes home," Nancy said. "If she sees this, she'll freak. I don't want her worrying about it until she has to. This just fries me," she said. "I know they're trying to scare me, and they have. But they're also making me very angry."

After Ned had left, Nancy forced herself to calm down so Hannah wouldn't notice that anything was wrong and ask questions. In her room, she turned on the TV, then snapped it off, put a tape in the deck, then immediately took it out. When Hannah came home, Nancy told her that she wanted some fresh air. She got in her car and went for a drive.

Nancy automatically turned toward the club. She didn't know what she was going to do there, but maybe she'd be able to get inside and explore—look in the lockers as Ned had suggested.

As Nancy was driving down the tree-lined entry drive toward the clubhouse, she thought of something that startled her. Her house hadn't been broken into. The door was just ajar, but it hadn't been jimmied, and neither had any of the windows. She was positive now that she *had* locked the door, so the only way anyone could have gotten in was with a key.

Nancy took her foot off the gas and let the car coast to a stop. She needed a minute to think it through. If the thief had used a key to get into her house, then maybe he had had keys for the other houses. But how?

Sitting in the car, Nancy went over her day—what she'd done and where she'd been. She had had her keys in her canvas bag, and the bag was with her the whole time.

Except, she remembered, when she had been in the weight room and when she had been having her massage. The bag had been in a locker then. Could someone have taken the key, made a copy, and put it back? Easy! After all, someone *had* put the note in her bag. Could it have been Cindy? Cindy certainly knew her way around the club.

Nancy thought of Rita, too. Could she have done it? Rita had never left the room. But Nancy remembered suddenly that she *had* made a short phone call.

What had she said? Something about being too busy to make it that night. Nancy thought she must have been canceling a date or something, and maybe she was. But maybe it was some kind of signal to let a partner know that Nancy's key was in a locker, there for the taking. Who could the partner be?

Nancy slowly backed her car up and out onto the main road. She drove about half a block until she came to a place where she could park so it would be half-hidden by trees. Then she walked through the grounds to the clubhouse. She decided it had been foolish to alert anyone that she was there by going up the driveway.

The clubhouse was dark and appeared to be locked up tight. But Nancy got lucky and found one open door. There were two choices: someone had forgotten to lock it, or someone was inside. Cautiously, she pushed the door open and stepped into the cool, dark silence.

Once inside, Nancy slipped off her sandals. She wished she weren't wearing a white top—it stood out like a neon light—but there was nothing she could do about it then. Taking a deep breath, she moved deeper into the building. Except for the occasional spill of moonlight slanting in from the windows, the club was night-dark. The silence was broken only by the faint ticking of a distant clock.

Bypassing the lounge, Nancy headed for the stairs that led to the locker rooms. She wanted to check out the locker she'd left her bag in to see how someone could have gotten in, left her that message, and taken her key.

There were a couple of yellow light bulbs burning downstairs, and they washed the hall in a sickly mustard glow. Walking soundlessly on the cool tiles, Nancy passed the locked women's massage room, the boiler room, and then turned into the locker room.

Using the weak glow from another yellow bulb, Nancy managed to find the locker she had used earlier. The key was in it, the same key she'd locked it with and kept in the pocket of her shorts. Most of the other lockers had keys in them, too.

That had to be it—the keys were interchangeable. Nancy took one out and tried it on another locker. No—it didn't work. Somebody must have used a key to get into the locker, though. Women went in and out of the room all day, and she couldn't imagine anyone taking the time to actually break into a locker. It was just too risky. Duplicate keys—

A faint sound. A bare foot on the tiles? Nancy froze and strained to hear it again. Holding her breath, she waited. She heard a car horn in the distance and the buzz of an airplane, and finally she distinguished the thudding of her heart. Then the noise came again, and Nancy whirled around—her hands were up, ready.

But the locker room remained empty. No one was looming in the doorway; no one was lurking in the shadows by the sinks.

Then Nancy almost laughed. The light was dim, but she saw it—a shining drop of water hanging from one of the faucets, ready to fall. When it did, she heard the gentle *plop* and realized she had been frightened by a slow drip from a faucet.

Her breathing returned to normal again. Nancy turned back to the lockers, thinking through her theory. The robber or robbers learn when a wealthy person will be away. Then they steal the person's house key from a locker room and have a duplicate made. But where do they copy the key? she wondered. They'd have to do it in the clubhouse; they wouldn't have time to take it away. And what about alarms at the houses? How could they break in without setting them off?

The faucet dripped again, an incredibly loud sound for such a small drop of water, and Nancy jumped again. Deciding she had had enough of the locker room, she stepped out into the still hallway. As she started toward the stairs, she noticed that the weight room door was open. As long as she was there, she decided, she might as well check it out, too.

Except for the spill of light from the hall bulbs, the weight room was all in shadow. The equipment, especially the big new weight-training machine, looked like monsters designed by a science-fiction writer.

Nancy walked into the middle of the room and realized that without a flashlight she wouldn't be able to detect much. Deciding to check out the room the next day, she turned to leave but paused by the new machine when she heard a noise that made her heart miss a beat. It wasn't water this time. It was a creaking sound with a faint jingling for accompaniment. The second sound was like the rattling of keys.

You've got keys on your mind, she told herself. As she took another step, the creaking-jingling sounded again. Nancy stopped and caught sight of the weight-training machine's shadow thrown high against the wall. The heavy piece of equipment was rocking slowly back and forth. But not by itself. Another shadow was next to it—the shadow of a person, both hands gripping the equipment, making the machine rock faster and faster. And as Nancy stood there, she realized that the machine was about to topple—straight onto her.

Chapter

Twelve

THERE WAS NO time to wonder who was pushing the machine. There was almost no time to move. But Nancy did, leaping sideways, trying to throw herself out of the path of that lethal piece of equipment. She had no idea how much it weighed, but she did know that if it hit her, she could be killed.

With a thud, Nancy hit the hard floor, her shoulder and head skidding on the rough, scratchy carpet. At the same moment, the state-of-the-art workout equipment crashed. It bounced once, crashed again, and then rocked back and forth more and more slowly. Finally, with a creak and a clank, it stopped.

Slowly, Nancy opened her eyes and looked. Less than five inches lay between the tip of her nose and the top of the heavy equipment. If she hadn't seen the shadows on the wall, she'd have been pinned to the floor right then, beneath hundreds of pounds of bone-crushing equipment.

Nancy was just sitting up when she heard the door to the weight room slam and the echo of feet padding quickly down the hall. The contents of the room became obscure without the light from the hall. Knowing she couldn't possibly follow in time, Nancy closed her eyes and fell back on the dusty carpet.

No one could have known I was coming here tonight, she told herself. But somebody saw me, and the minute he did, I almost got caught.

Disgusted with herself for not being quieter and more careful, Nancy rolled quickly away from the workout equipment and started to get to her knees. That was when she noticed a narrow door in the wall next to her. Probably some kind of storage place, she thought. But then she remembered that the storage closet was on the opposite wall.

Nancy tested the metal handle. Locked, naturally. She knew she should get out of there and go home, but she couldn't stop wondering about what was behind that door. A set of duplicate keys for all the lockers, maybe? Or, better yet, a diamond and ruby necklace, a Picasso painting, a rare book, and all the other things that had been stolen?

After she opened the door to the hallway, she could see better. She rummaged in her large straw handbag for her lock-picking kit. She wished she could turn on a light, but she didn't dare risk it. Moving the small picks in the lock, she turned the tumblers by feel and sound.

A few minutes later, Nancy was staring at two packages of light bulbs, a small pile of rags, and, behind these, a void. Not much of a storage closet, she thought. She pushed the bulbs and rags aside and stepped in, stretching her hands out in front of her. She expected to be stopped by a back wall, but instead she continued to feel only air. She kept going, sure that she'd hit a wall any second—but nothing. She was in a long, narrow passageway.

As Nancy walked farther into the corridor, her hands felt nothing but the two walls on either side of her—no boxes, no spare equipment, nothing. It wouldn't be a very good storage room, anyway, she thought. It was so long and narrow that it would take hours to get anything from the back.

Nancy took a few more steps, then stumbled as her foot hit what felt like a loose tile. Instinctively, she threw her arms out to the sides to steady herself in the pitch darkness. But instead of hitting solid wall, her right hand pushed against a flimsy piece of metal that swung in silently and smoothly.

After Nancy regained her balance, she felt around with her hands, trying to figure out what kind of cabinet she had opened. She touched something soft and slightly damp. Pulling it out, she discovered that it was a terry-cloth towel. As she put her hand back into the cabinet—or whatever it was—she saw thin yellow lines of light spilling faintly into the cabinet. Her fingers reached out and closed around a plastic bottle; she removed it, opened it, and sniffed. It was suntan lotion.

A towel, a bottle of lotion, and yellow light. This isn't just any cabinet, Nancy thought excitedly. She was looking into the rear of a locker.

Wanting to make certain, she stepped back, ran her hands along the wall for a few inches, and then pushed again. Another metal panel swung in, and more lines of yellow light from the locker room fell into the locker. The same thing happened on the left wall.

It was perfect, Nancy thought with a smile. A perfectly beautiful setup. The door in the weight room, the little stash of light bulbs to make people think it was for storage, and the long line of locker backs, cleverly fixed so they could be opened and the robbers could help themselves to anyone's house keys. People in the locker rooms would not even be aware that one of the lockers was being rifled.

Nancy pushed open a few more locker backs. Even if she didn't know who was committing the burglaries, she at least knew how. And that meant she was one step closer to putting all the pieces together.

Nancy closed the metal panels and headed down the passageway and back into the weight room. As she passed the workout machine, lying still like some large wounded animal, she almost laughed. Whoever had pushed it at her had actually ended up helping her to crack the case! She was on to their secret now, and it was only a matter of time before she had them trapped!

Nancy gave the machine a pat, then gathered up her bag and the sandals she had dropped when she made her flying leap. She'd just left the weight room and was walking down the hall toward the stairs when a clattering noise made her spin around.

The noise went on for a few seconds. It sounded like rocks tumbling in a washing machine. Nancy saw that she was standing right next to the boiler room door. She pushed it open, and the noise got louder before settling down to a steady hum.

The pipes must be rattling, Nancy thought, or maybe the air conditioner had come on. Boiler rooms always had equipment that made loud noises. In the daytime, she wouldn't even have noticed it. And neither would anyone else, she thought suddenly.

On a hunch, Nancy stepped into the room and began looking around. In just five minutes, her hunch paid off. Stuck in a far corner, behind a pile of old pipes and covered with a dusty canvas sheet, was another piece of equipment. When Nancy pulled the sheet off, she found herself looking at a key-duplicating machine.

Perfect, she thought again. Anyone hearing the key duplicator would think it was just the furnace or the pipes and wouldn't check to see what the noise was.

Nancy had just left the boiler room when another sound made her freeze. Voices were coming from somewhere above her in the clubhouse. She couldn't tell exactly how many, but one was a man's, and at least one belonged to a woman. The robbers, she decided, coming back to check if the weight machine had done its work.

Quietly but quickly, Nancy padded barefoot the rest of the way down the hall, then ran lightly up the stairs. At the top of the stairs, she stopped, held her breath, and listened. The voices were coming from the lounge. She could hear them perfectly now, and what she heard made her burst out laughing. Fooled again, Detective, she told herself.

In the lounge sat Bess, George, and two boys Nancy didn't recognize. They were laughing, drinking soda, and obviously enjoying having the place to themselves. When Bess saw Nancy standing in the doorway, she jumped.

"Nan!" she said, surprised. "You scared me. What are you doing here?"

"I—I was looking for something. But now that I'm here, I think maybe I'll join the party," Nancy answered with a smile.

"Well, come on in!" the boy sitting next to Bess called out. He had brown hair and a very good build, and Nancy figured he must be Tom, the "gorgeous" caddy.

As Nancy took a chair at the round table,

George reached into a cooler and pulled out a can of soda. "Here," she said, sliding the soda to Nancy. "Jim and I brought these along, and they're still nice and cold."

Smiling at Jim, the tennis instructor, Nancy popped open the can and took a sip. "What is this? A late-night picnic?"

"Yeah," Tom said. "We ran into each other at Frank's Pizza, but it was so packed, it was sardine city. So we decided to come here to make our plans."

"Plans?"

"For tomorrow," Jim said. "It's the Fourth of July, and the club always has a big bash."

"We were just trying to decide how we're going to get together," Bess explained.

"When did you get here?" Nancy asked, suddenly changing the subject.

"Oh, about ten, fifteen minutes ago," Tom said.

"You didn't happen to see anyone leaving, did you?" Nancy asked. "Maybe somebody in a hurry?"

George shook her head. "The place was empty when we got here. I didn't even want to come in, but Jim said it was okay."

"The staff's allowed," Jim explained.

"So I've heard," Nancy said, wondering if it had been a member of the staff who had tried to bury her under a muscle-building machine.

It couldn't be Tom or Jim, at least she knew that for sure now, and she could scratch them off her list.

"Nan?" Bess broke into her thoughts. "What do you think? Should we all dress up in red, white, and blue for tomorrow?"

"It sounds kind of silly," George said.

"That's the idea," Tom said. "Everybody gets silly around here on the Fourth. But it's fun—you should see the fireworks display. It's amazing."

"Well, I'm going to wear a red, white, and blue hat, at least," Bess said, deciding out loud. Looking around the lounge, she laughed. "Hey, you know, this is the first time I've spent any time in here. I think I'll come more often."

"That's it!" Nancy said.

"What's it?"

"That's what you'll do." Turning to Bess, she grinned. "How'd you like to spend tomorrow here, in and around the clubhouse?" she asked. "You could swim and lounge around by the pool, you could have cold lemonade anytime you wanted, you could have a massage—"

"Sounds great!" Bess answered.

"There are only two things you have to do," Nancy said. "You have to have one short, easy little workout session in the weight room. And you have to talk. A lot."

"I think I can manage that," Bess said with a laugh. "Talking's one of my specialties."

The two guys looked completely confused, but Bess and George knew exactly what Nancy was up to. It was time for her to set a trap.

Chapter

Thirteen

THE NEXT MORNING, Nancy shaded her eyes and looked up from her lounger beside the club pool. A sleek red Jaguar had just sped up the entry drive and swerved quickly into a parking spot near the clubhouse.

As Nancy and at least a dozen other people watched, Bess Marvin climbed out of the car, pulled out a designer-initialed duffel bag, adjusted her expensive-looking sunglasses, flipped back her shining blond hair, and sauntered slowly toward the pool.

Good, Nancy thought, smiling to herself.

Bess has everyone's attention. Now, let's see who's going to be the most interested in what she has to say.

"My gosh, it's crowded out here!" Bess exclaimed as she flopped into a chair not too close to Nancy's. "Is this the only patio?"

"Well, it is the Fourth. But we've been arguing for two years about expanding it," someone said. "Didn't you get the bulletins?"

"I just moved here," Bess explained. "We joined the club a week ago. I've been on the golf course, but this is the first chance I've had to use the pool. And would you believe it, the whole family's leaving town again tomorrow for a week."

"Well, on behalf of the staff, let me welcome you." Poor Mike was on duty again. He leaned down from his lifeguard chair and smiled, obviously attracted to Bess. "I hope you'll spend more time here once you get back."

Fingering what looked like a small teardrop diamond at the end of a silver chain around her neck, Bess smiled back. "Thanks," she said, and her hand reached up to touch one of her earrings. It flashed like a jewel in the sunlight, but like the necklace, it was a fake. A good one, but paste nonetheless. "That water looks absolutely wonderful," Bess went on, gazing at the pool. "If somebody will tell me where the safe is, I'll just get rid of my jewelry and go for a swim."

"Safe?" Mike laughed. "There isn't any safe."

Bess looked amazed, as if she'd never heard of such a thing. "But where do people put their jewelry when they want to go in the water?"

"Most people leave it at home," somebody else said.

"Oh, well, I leave the really valuable things at home," Bess said. "I mean, there are some things that never come out of our wall safe in the library. But this?" She held out the necklace and gave a little laugh. "This is just everyday stuff."

"Then don't worry about it," Mike told her. "Just put it in one of the lockers. It'll be there when you get back."

Looking skeptical, Bess stood up and walked into the lounge. Nancy waited a few minutes and then followed her, but just to the doorway. She wanted to keep a very low profile that day.

Ned, George, and two of Ned's friends —one of whom owned the red Jaguar—were sitting at a table, laughing and talking. Nancy had wanted Ned and George to be there to keep an eye on Bess.

Bess had stopped at the bar and ordered an

iced tea. Max Fletcher was sitting next to her, and Bess immediately struck up a conversation with him. Nancy grinned. Trust Bess to find time to talk to a handsome guy.

Finally, Bess turned to the woman next to her and spoke loudly enough for Nancy to hear. "What a beautiful emerald!" she exclaimed, peering closely at the ring on the woman's hand. "And what a beautiful setting. I've never seen one like it before."

The woman laughed, pleased at the compliment. "That's because there isn't another one like it. This is one of a kind. An old family heirloom."

"Oh, one of those. My mother has some of the most gorgeous pieces of jewelry, and they've been handed down, too. Someday they'll be mine." Bess sighed. "Unfortunately, they're all in the library safe, and that's where they'll stay until I'm twenty-one."

"Well, that won't be too long, will it?" the woman asked.

"No, but the thing is, we're going on vacation tomorrow," Bess told her. "We'll be spending an entire week with a bunch of people I've never met, and I'd love to make a fantastic impression. There's this strand of pearls with a diamond clasp that would really dazzle them."

The woman smiled, and Nancy tried not to laugh out loud. Bess was doing a perfect job. Practically the entire club now thought that she came from a wealthy family that had a safe full of valuable one-of-a-kind pieces of jewelry. And the most important thing was that they thought her house would be empty for a week. If nobody bites, Nancy thought, I might as well give up being a detective completely.

Bess turned back to Max Fletcher and started talking to him, not so loudly this time. Satisfied that things were going right, Nancy left. She had just passed the pool and was heading for the other side of the clubhouse when a girl with flaming red curls stepped out and hesitated in front of her. It was Cindy.

Nancy stopped, waiting to see what Cindy was up to.

Finally, after nervously clearing her throat, Cindy said, "I have to talk to you."

"I think that's a good idea," Nancy said.

"I want you to know that I put Mrs. Ames's watch back about an hour ago," Cindy said. "She's out by the pool. You can ask her. She's probably found it by now."

"It's nice that you put it back," Nancy said. "Is there anything else you have to return?"

Cindy looked confused and then angry as the implication of what Nancy said sunk in.

"What are you talking about?" she asked. "I never took anything else."

"Well, you took the watch. Why shouldn't I think you'd take other things?"

"Because I didn't, that's why!" Cindy cried. "Look, the watch is the only *thing* I've ever taken. All the other times it's just been money that people have left in their bags."

"All the other times?" Nancy asked.

Cindy nodded. "I know it's wrong, but I can't help it. It's like a game." She swallowed and pushed back her hair. "Anyway, when you saw me that time, I realized that the game was up. I put the watch back, and I promised myself I'd get help so I won't steal things anymore."

Nancy and Cindy stared at each other. Cindy seemed to be telling the truth, but how could she know for sure? Cindy dropped her eyes and backed away.

Just then, Ned and George came around the corner. "Nan," Ned said quietly. "Bess is just about to make her next move. You said you wanted to be there."

"I do." Still watching Cindy as she walked farther away, Nancy said to Ned, "I'll go into the clubhouse. You two stick with Cindy, okay? Don't let her out of your sight."

If Cindy's in on it, Nancy thought as she

headed back to the lounge, then she won't be able to warn anyone. And if she's the only thief, then we've got her.

The lounge was still extremely busy. It seemed as if every member of the club had turned out that day for the big Fourth of July party.

Extra waiters had been hired, and Nancy had trouble squeezing herself in at a busy table to order an iced tea from one of them. Zach was still behind the bar, she noticed, and Bess was just winding up her conversation with Max Fletcher.

"Well," Bess was saying, "since I do want to impress those people, I suppose I'd better get down to the weight room. I should have started working out a week ago—there's no way I'll lose five pounds in one session."

With a smile, Bess left the bar and sauntered slowly toward the stairway leading to the lower level. Nancy drank some of her tea, but she barely tasted it. This was the most important part of the trap. Bess was going to do a short workout, then have a massage. But before she went in with Rita, she was going to deposit her bag in a locker. If Nancy's plan worked, then somebody would use that little passageway to get to Bess's house key. If the thief was Cindy, then nothing would happen. But if the redhead *wasn't* the one, Nancy would catch the person right in the act.

At first, Nancy had planned to hide in the passageway or the boiler room. But that wouldn't be enough, she decided. She needed to catch someone actually going into Bess's house with the copy of the key they had made that day. She needed irrefutable proof.

Bess was gone by then. Nancy looked around to see if she could spot anything or anyone and that was when she saw Mike. He was standing in the doorway to the lounge, and he was looking toward the staircase.

This is it, Nancy thought excitedly. He's the one! He's going to follow her downstairs to see what she does. And when she puts her bag into a locker, he'll go into action.

Casually waving to a few people in the lounge, Mike strolled toward the stairway. Nancy waited until he had passed her table. Then she stood up and turned toward the stairs herself.

Zach was standing in front of her, his dark eyes twinkling as if he were really happy to see her.

"Hi, Nancy. Have you seen Joanna lately? She hasn't been around."

"Yes. I mean, no, I haven't seen her lately." Nancy looked past him, not wanting to lose sight of Mike, even though she knew where he was going. Then she smiled at Zach. "Sorry. I'm in kind of a hurry."

"Oh, no, I'm sorry. I almost forgot," he said. "You've got a phone call."

"Me?" Who'd be calling me here? Nancy wondered.

"That's right."

Mike had gone down the stairs then. "But there must be a mistake," she said. "Nobody knows I'm here."

"Somebody does," Zach told her and pulled on her elbow. "They asked for you. Come on. I said, 'Come on.' There's a phone at the bar. Take it there."

As he spoke, Zach had been propelling her gently but with authority ahead of him. She wondered about his behavior, but for just a minute. It was the worst possible time for a phone call. She'd miss Mike. Besides, she'd never be able to hear—the bar was three deep in people.

Just as she reached the bar, a sudden realization hit Nancy. Zach was purposely trying to keep her from following Mike. Could he be in on it, too? He has to be, Nancy thought. And he did practically shove me over here.

Nancy turned and faced Zach. He was still smiling, but his eyes weren't twinkling as they usually did. She forced herself to smile back.

She didn't want to let him know that she suspected him. It was much too soon.

Calmly, Nancy moved past the crowd and walked behind the bar to pick up the phone.

"Hello, Nancy," a female voice said. "I see you decided not to take our advice and get off the case."

Although she tried to disguise it, the voice belonged to Rita!

Chapter
Fourteen

NANCY TOOK A slow, deep breath, hoping her voice wouldn't shake when she accused the person on the other end. "Hello, Rita," she said, surprisingly steadily.

"You couldn't stay away, could you?" Rita asked, dropping her disguise. "You just had to keep on trying to help your little friend, Joanna."

"Right," Nancy said. "Well, Rita, it's been nice talking to you, but I've really got to hang up now."

"Nice try," Rita said with a laugh. "But, Nancy dear, here's what's really going to happen. First, say goodbye to anyone you know at the bar in a real friendly way. We don't want anyone suspecting anything."

Nancy glanced over at the door leading to the pool, hoping to see Ned or George out there. No luck. She had told them to stay with Cindy, and that's exactly what they were doing.

"And then," Rita continued, "you'll do exactly what Zach tells you to do."

"What if I don't?" Nancy asked.

Rita laughed her usual friendly laugh. "Why don't you take a look at everybody's favorite bartender?" she suggested.

Nancy looked. Zach was standing right beside her. In one hand, he held a glass of soda. But in the other hand, hidden from everyone's view but Nancy's, was a gun, pointed straight at her. When he saw her notice the gun, Zach winked.

"Okay, I've seen it," Nancy told Rita. "What are you telling me? That if I don't do what he says, he'll shoot me? Right here in front of all these witnesses? That's pretty hard to believe."

"Well, you're welcome to put him to the test," Rita said. And she didn't laugh this time. "But I guarantee you'll be very disappointed."

For a second, Nancy was tempted to call

their bluff, if it was a bluff. But then she looked at the gun again and saw that its barrel was longer than usual. Looking more closely, she realized that it wasn't an extralong barrel; it was a normal barrel with a silencer on the end of it. The lounge was so crowded and noisy that a gunshot would sound about as loud as a pin dropping on the carpet.

"All right," Nancy said to Rita. "You win. For now, anyway. What do you want me to do?"

Rita chuckled. "As I said, do whatever Zach tells you. And no tricks, Nancy, or you'll be very sorry."

I'm sorry already, Nancy thought, hanging up the phone. Turning to Zach, she said, "Well? What's the plan?"

For an answer, Zach draped a dishtowel over his wrist, concealing the gun. Then he nodded toward the direction of the locker room stairs. "I'll be right behind you," he said, smiling so that everyone would think he was enjoying the company of a pretty girl. "Let's move, Nancy, okay?"

As slowly as she could, Nancy walked toward the stairs. But it wasn't slow enough. Ned and George didn't suddenly appear in the lounge to help her. No one even paid any attention as the two of them went down to the lower level.

As they walked along the hall, they passed the weight room, and out of the corner of her eye Nancy saw Bess. Her friend was on the rowing machine, going nowhere very slowly. It was easy to see that Bess was bored—she kept glancing around the room. Nancy was tempted to wave to get Bess's attention. Maybe Bess would see Zach, realize that something was wrong, and go for help. But just as she was about to raise her hand, Nancy felt something on her back. She was wearing a thin cotton top, and what she felt was cold and hard —Zach was pushing her ahead with the gun.

The hallway was empty. If Nancy was going to make a move, she knew she had to do it then. Pretending to stumble, she whirled around, aimed her left foot at Zach's gun hand, and kicked. The gun went flying, landing at the bottom of the stairs. Nancy started to race toward it and then stopped.

At the bottom of the stairs stood Max Fletcher. He bent down and calmly picked up the gun. He aimed it at Nancy. "Walk," he said softly. Nancy had no choice but to turn around and walk.

A few more feet, and they were at the door to the massage room. Max motioned with the gun, and Zach roughly pushed Nancy inside, then closed and locked the door behind them.

Rita was waiting. At the sight of Max, she

looked slightly surprised. Not as surprised as I am, Nancy thought.

"Don't be too hard on yourself, Nancy," Max said with a chuckle. "Except for ignoring me, you've been very clever. Of course, you wasted some valuable time with the lifeguard and that redheaded kleptomaniac." He chuckled again. "But there was no reason for you to suspect me. After all, I never did anything suspicious. And I'm a very wealthy man. Sole owner of Fletcher Electronics, a multimillion-dollar company that manufactures, among other things, the Fletcher Home Alarm System and wall safes. Maybe you've heard of them?"

Nancy stared at him. Now she knew why the name of his company had rung a bell when Joanna mentioned it. Fletcher alarms and safes were all over the place—in houses, office buildings, even cars. Home alarm systems, she thought. No wonder they were able to break into those houses without problems. Max Fletcher wouldn't have any trouble dismantling his own product. And if a house used a different system, well, that wouldn't stop him, either. He probably knew the competition's alarms as well as he knew his own.

"But why?" Nancy asked. "You have enough money."

"The challenge, Nancy," he said. "The excitement. Fletcher Electronics is boring.

Haven't you ever been so bored you'd do anything for excitement?"

Nancy didn't answer.

"Fortunately," Max said, "Rita and Zach shared my enthusiasm for a challenge, and I had no trouble getting them to join in my scheme. But, now that you know it all, I'm afraid we have to stop you."

Calmly, Max handed the gun to Zach. Then, with a nod and a smile to Nancy, he left the room.

She looked around quickly, hoping to spot a way out. Rita laughed. "Don't bother," she said. "There's only one way in and one way out, and Zach's covering it."

Nancy looked at Zach, who was leaning against the door, pointing the gun at her. Then she looked back at Rita. "Well," she said. "What now?"

"Let's get it over with, Rita," Zach said. "The sooner the better."

"Don't worry," Rita told him. "We have plenty of time." She smiled at Nancy. "I have to tell you, you really had us hopping for a while. We tried everything—the shower, the diving pool, the messages, the weight machine, but you wouldn't stop."

"Hey, Rita." Zach seemed very edgy. "I don't think Max wanted us to chat. Let's get this over with and get out of here."

Desperately, Nancy tried to stall for time. "I know you two could call each other on your phones to say when to get a key. But I hate to admit it, there's one thing I haven't figured out yet."

"I don't believe it," Rita said sarcastically. "The great girl detective doesn't have all the answers?"

"Not quite," Nancy said. "I don't know where you put the things you stole. So as long as you're going to seal my lips permanently, why don't you tell me? I'm dying of curiosity —excuse the pun."

Rita started to answer, but Zach broke in. "Okay, that's enough," he said to Rita. "Max left me in charge of this part of the operation, and I say we wrap it up and hit the road."

"Oh?" Nancy asked. "You're leaving town?"

"That's right," Rita said. "The River Heights Country Club has been very good to us, but you know what they say about too much of a good thing. Max says it's time to move on."

"Yeah, but there's just one thing we have to do before we leave," Zach said.

Rita nodded. "That's right," she said sadly, as if she really cared. "We're going to have to do something about you, Nancy."

"I don't suppose you'd believe me if I said I'd keep my mouth shut." Nancy could tell that Zach was getting edgier by the second, and she wanted to keep the conversation going. Anything to keep him from "wrapping it up."

"No, I wouldn't believe you for a minute," Rita told her. She was moving around the room now, closing cabinet doors and checking to make sure she hadn't left anything behind. "I'm surprised you'd even say anything as phony as that."

Nancy tried to laugh again. "Well, you can't blame me for trying. But since it didn't work, I think I ought to tell you that I do have friends here helping me. And if I don't meet them soon, they'll come looking for me. If they don't find me, they'll know something's wrong, and then you'll have the police breathing down your necks."

But Rita didn't seem threatened at all. "The police?" she said, raising her eyebrows skeptically. "The police were here once and went away empty-handed. Besides, we'll be long gone when they find you. And at that point, I'm afraid you won't be able to tell them a thing."

"Rita, will you just shut up!" Zach cried hoarsely. "If you keep running your mouth, somebody's going to turn up here."

Zach had obviously had enough, and Nancy knew that if she wanted to make a break for it, this was the time. She slowly took a step forward as if to follow Zach, then suddenly whirled around and started to swing the side of her hand down on Zach's arm.

But Zach was ready for her. Before Nancy could finish her move, he had dropped the gun and pinned her arms to her sides. Lifting her up, he tossed her onto the massage table and held her down, one hand over her mouth.

"My, my, Nancy, you're very tense," Rita said, clucking her tongue sympathetically. "You're lucky, though. I know all about relaxing tight muscles."

Nancy looked on helplessly as Rita moved to the table. Next she felt Rita's fingers tightening around her neck.

Nancy squirmed, twisting her body and shaking her head as hard as she could. She felt Zach's hand slip and immediately bit him on the thumb. He gasped and took his hand away. Nancy opened her mouth to scream.

"Don't do it!" Zach ordered, his dark eyes inches from hers. "One sound out of you and, believe me, I'll use this!"

Out of the corner of her eye, Nancy saw the gun—it was pointed straight at her temple. She closed her mouth.

"That's better," Rita said.

Again, Nancy felt Rita's fingers on her neck, then a sharp pain, and finally nothing.

Chapter

Fifteen

Slowly, Nancy turned her head and opened her eyes. It was as black as when she had them closed. Her head ached, and she wanted to raise her hand to rub it. But she couldn't move her hands because they were tied behind her. Nancy then realized that her feet were tied also. She started to yell but discovered that her mouth had been taped.

One corner of the tape was loose, though, and by rubbing the edge against her shoulder, Nancy was able to peel it off. She shouted, but the only reply was the echo of her own voice.

Instinctively, Nancy began to struggle against the bindings that held her. All of her pulling and twisting only succeeding in scraping raw spots on her wrists and ankles.

Stop it, she told herself after a minute. Panicking won't get you anywhere. Breathe normally, and be thankful you're alive.

Nancy managed to calm herself and lay still on what felt like a hard floor. Her wrists and ankles were sore, and her head still ached, but otherwise she was fine. Which was weird, she thought, since the last thing she had seen before blacking out was the wrong end of a gun pointing at her head.

So Zach and Rita hadn't really meant to shoot her. Not right there in the massage room, anyway. Rita must have found some nerve in her neck that was guaranteed to send her straight to sleep. A pretty good trick, Nancy admitted. I'll have to learn that one myself someday.

But why hadn't Max wanted her killed yet? Nancy wondered. Well, of course, it was obvious. They could hardly haul a body through the crowded country club. They had stashed her someplace, and when they were good and ready, they'd come back and "wrap it up," as Zach had said.

That must mean I'm still at the club, Nancy thought. It would be too hard to get me out of here dead or unconscious. There are just too many people around.

But where in the club was she? Was she still downstairs, maybe in the massage room? It was possible. Rita could have closed up for the day and gone to join the holiday crowd.

Nancy tried to see anything that would give her a clue to where she was. The cabinets in the massage room were gleaming white metal, she remembered, and the tables were covered with white pads. Her eyes should have adjusted enough by then to see white, even with the lights off. But all she saw were black and dark shades of gray.

Cautiously, Nancy tested her wrists and ankles again. The ropes seemed to have loosened a little; she might be able to get free if she didn't rub her skin raw.

Moving slowly, Nancy sat up with her legs out in front of her. She decided to try to slip her arms under her legs and then shove her feet through the loop her arms made. That way, her arms would be in front of her, and she could untie her feet.

Digging at the knots with her fingernails, Nancy did eventually loosen them. When her legs were free, she discovered that they had gone to sleep, and she kicked them to get the circulation moving. Her foot struck something metallic.

She reached out with her feet again, and this time the metal gave a little. She scooted closer to the wall and shoved her foot against it as hard as she could. The cover moved as if it were on hinges.

As it flapped open, Nancy noticed thin lines of yellow light leaking in. When she realized what it was, she felt like smiling. She was looking through the back end of a locker. Zach and Rita had put her in the passageway between the locker rooms.

But suddenly, Nancy didn't feel like smiling. The time must be getting very close to when they would come back for her. The yellow light meant that it was night. The locker rooms and weight room were closed for the day. Nobody would be interested in using them, anyway; they were all outside, dancing and eating and waiting for the fireworks. No wonder no one had heard her when she yelled.

Max and Rita and Zach were probably up there, too, Nancy realized. And once the big bash was over and the club was deserted, they'd come for her. She didn't know exactly what they had in mind, but she had a feeling she'd be found the next day at the bottom of the swimming pool or out on the golf course, the victim of an accidental drowning or a bad fall. Of course, Ned and Bess and George would tell the police about her investigation.

But they wouldn't know whom she suspected. And by the time they figured it out, those two would be gone. And Max would be back at the tennis courts, making bets on games. He'd never be caught. He could even wait awhile, recruit more people to help him, and then start his whole operation all over again. I'm the only one who knows, Nancy thought. I'm the only one who can stop him.

Aware that she didn't have much time, Nancy bit down on the ropes holding her wrists and began pulling at the knots. The task was too difficult, and she felt like weeping. But then she remembered the light bulbs. She stood and walked down the passageway until she reached the end. It was the wrong end, though. Turning around, she worked her way back until she stumbled into the light bulbs stacked in front of the weight room door.

Breaking a bulb against the wall, Nancy put the base of it into her mouth and sawed at the rope on her wrists with the jagged, broken glass. Eventually, the rope frayed, and she pulled her hands free.

The door to the weight room was locked, naturally. But Nancy banged on it a few times, hoping that someone might hear her. No one came.

On her hands and knees again, Nancy felt around the floor, hoping to come across something she could use to pick the lock. She turned around and crawled in the other direction, sweeping her hands across the floor in front of her. By the time she reached the far end, she had picked up nothing but a lot of dust.

Nancy sat down and leaned back against the end wall, trying to decide what to do next. She heard something. Sitting up straighter, she listened closely. There it was again—the sound of cheering and clapping. Could the fireworks have started already? If they had, then time was really running out. She listened again. People were still laughing and cheering, but she didn't hear the pop or whine of firecrackers. They were probably just clapping for the music and laughing at their own jokes. Now, if she could just find a way to get out, she could join them.

Frustrated, Nancy banged at one of the locker backs with her fist. It swung in smoothly, just like all the others. Inside, she saw a pale blob of something. Pulling it out, she discovered it was a pair of much-used sweat socks. She started to stuff them back in and then realized how stupid she was being.

These are lockers, you idiot, she told herself. *Storage* lockers. Find something like a belt buckle or a barrette, and you just might be out of here.

Five minutes later, Nancy was a quarter of the way down the passage, rifling what must have been her fiftieth locker. So far, she had found a belt with the wrong kind of buckle, a deck of playing cards that were too flimsy to wedge open the lock, several combs and brushes, three dozen tennis balls, and enough dirty towels to start a laundry service. But she hadn't found anything that would help her get out.

Just keep going, Nancy told herself. There has to be something in one of these lockers that I can use. After all, people leave their keys in them; maybe they leave their credit cards, too. Or maybe a pocket knife or a nail clipper.

Pushing open yet another locker back, Nancy dragged out the usual wadded-up towel and then stretched her arm deep inside, hoping that this time she'd be lucky.

Suddenly, there was a screech of metal, and the thin lines of yellow light grew wide. Nancy's eyes had become so used to the dark by then that she squinted as if a floodlight had been turned on. Then she finally realized that the locker door had been yanked open—from inside the locker room. Before she had a chance to react, a hand had closed over her wrist, the fingers tightening in a powerful grip.

Chapter
Sixteen

NANCY TRIED TO pull her arm back, but the hand only grasped tighter, the fingers digging into her arm and pushing it painfully against the sharp metal lip of the locker.

It would probably do her no good, but Nancy yelled, anyway.

"Hey!" a voice cried out. "Pipe down. This place is like an echo chamber, and you're breaking my ear drums!"

Ignoring the voice, Nancy started to yell again, and then a flashlight blinded her. Gasping, she put her free hand over her eyes.

"Well, well," the voice said. "You do get

yourself into the strangest predicaments, Ms. Drew."

Nancy gasped again, not because of the light but because she had suddenly recognized the voice. It was Detective John Ryan's.

Nancy let out her breath in relief. She wouldn't have to go poking through any more lockers, and she wouldn't be the victim of some "tragic accident" after all. She was safe.

After a moment, though, she realized that Ryan was still gripping her wrist and shining the flashlight in her eyes. She was relieved and happy that he was there, but she couldn't help feeling annoyed with him.

"Since you know who I am," she said, "why don't you stop trying to break my arm? And while you're at it, you might turn that flashlight off. I've been in this dungeon for hours, and my eyes have become very sensitive."

The detective immediately let go of her wrist and turned the flashlight away from her eyes. Nancy could see the knot of his dark red tie and the cleft in his strongly shaped chin, but his handsome face was in shadow. Then she heard a dry, throaty sound, and she realized that he was giving his imitation of a laugh.

"I'm glad you're enjoying yourself," she said wryly. "Do you want to share the joke, or is it private?"

"I'm afraid it's very private, Ms. Drew," he said. "In fact, I'm laughing at myself."

"Oh?" Nancy was surprised. Detective Ryan didn't seem as if he were the kind of man who could laugh at himself.

He didn't explain, though, and Nancy decided not to waste any time asking about it. "Never mind about the joke—whatever it is. How did you find me?"

"I got a call," he said.

"An anonymous call?"

Nancy saw his head shake.

"No, this one was very un-anonymous," the detective said. "Three people called me, and they all identified themselves. Bess Marvin, George Fayne, and Ned Nickerson. I assume you know them all?"

Nancy smiled. "Yes, I know them," she said. "They're my friends, and they called you because they knew I was in trouble."

"So they said," Detective Ryan commented. "Well, you can't say I didn't warn you."

Nancy could hardly believe it. She'd been threatened with a gun, tied up, and thrown in a dark, dusty passageway, and all he could say was "I told you so." She took a deep breath. "Aren't you interested in what I've found out?"

The detective's head moved up and down in

a quick nod. Nancy decided he was just too proud to admit that she might have solved his case and that his nod was the only hint she'd ever get that he really did want to know what had been going on. Quickly, but without leaving out any important details, she told him everything.

"Fletcher Electronics," Detective Ryan said when she'd finished, sounding completely disgusted. "It was right in front of my eyes."

"Mine, too," Nancy said. "Anyway, all I care about now is catching those creeps. How about getting me out of here so we can do it?"

The detective nodded, and after Nancy told him about the door in the weight room, he had it open in about three minutes.

"I think I know what solitary confinement means now," Nancy said as she stepped into the weight room. "Thanks for getting me out."

"Right. So give me a description," Detective Ryan demanded.

Nancy sighed. The detective obviously wasn't going to apologize for ignoring her for so long or thank her for helping to solve his case. Well, she told herself, I guess that's not as important as catching the thieves.

"I'm waiting," he said.

Quickly, Nancy described Zach and Rita and Max. "Listen, I know you've got a job to do. But we could finish it together. I think we ought to try to cooperate, at least until it's over. Deal?"

"Deal," he said after a couple of seconds. Together, the two of them raced for the stairs.

When they reached the lounge, they stopped and checked to see if Zach was at his usual place behind the bar. He wasn't.

"I guess that would have been too easy," the detective remarked. "Let's start checking the rest of the place." Without waiting for Nancy, he headed for the sliding doors that led to the pool.

At first, Nancy was so glad to be outside, breathing fresh air, that she couldn't decide what to do or where to begin looking for the culprits. For a moment, she just stood still, enjoying her freedom. When a hand touched her arm, she jumped and yelped.

"Steady," Ned said, putting his arm around her shoulders. "I'm one of the good guys."

"That's for sure," Nancy said, hugging him. "Thanks for calling the detective. I wasn't sure how much longer I'd have before Rita and Zach came back for me."

"So it *is* those two," Ned said with a frown. "When that lifeguard came back outside, I gave him the third degree, but he had about fifty witnesses to prove that he'd just gone to the locker room for some zinc oxide for his nose. George stayed with Cindy the whole time, and the girl didn't try to make a move. I figured it must be the bartender, but by that time it was too late."

"It doesn't matter now," Nancy said. "But it's three people, not two. The third one is Max Fletcher, and he's the brains behind the whole thing. Tell George and Bess, so they can look for him, too."

"Right," Ned said. "I'm going to check downstairs again, just to make sure they didn't slip back in there while we weren't looking. You might as well look around outside, but it's not going to be easy, Nan. It's almost time for the fireworks, and this place is a madhouse."

"Don't worry," Nancy said. "If they're here, we'll find them."

After Ned took off, Nancy looked around again. Now she knew what he meant by madhouse. The lounge, the deck around the pool, parts of the golf course, every place was filled with people waiting for the fireworks to begin. They weren't waiting quietly, either. Some were milling around with paper plates in their hands, some were dancing, some were swimming, and they were all talking and laughing at the top of their lungs.

The whole area was lit by torches, and

Nancy knew she'd have trouble picking out specific faces in the flickering light, but she stepped into the crowd, anyway. They have to be here, she told herself. They were planning to come back for her when the party was over, and they wouldn't want to go too far while they waited. Besides, Zach was the bartender. He had a job to do. And if he wasn't doing it in the lounge, then he must be outside, passing around trays of drinks.

As Nancy was edging her way through a knot of people, someone put a hot dog in her hand. She gratefully ate it while she continued searching. She saw Detective Ryan over by the swimming pool and caught his eye. Shaking his head, he gave her a thumbs-down signal.

Turning around, Nancy walked back to the lounge door, hoping that maybe Zach had returned for a refill. He hadn't, but on the far side of the room she saw Bess and George. When they spotted her, they waved and smiled, glad to see that she was okay. Nancy quickly joined them and explained who the thieves were. But neither girl had seen them, so Nancy decided to move on to the golf course.

Wishing she had another hot dog, Nancy pushed her way through clumps of people and finally made it to the smooth grass of the golf course. She stopped a second to take off her sandals, just in case she had to do any running. Carrying them in her hand, she started wandering through the happy crowd, checking every face but never finding the right ones.

Suddenly, the noise of the crowd seemed to get even louder. A cheer went up, and everyone started clapping. A man said, "This is the biggest one ever. I bet they'll see it as far away as Chicago." Looking to where he was pointing—at a small hill just a short distance from the crowd—Nancy could see where the fireworks display had been set up, and she realized it was about to begin.

Frustrated, Nancy turned around, and that was when she saw them. Two of them, anyway. Standing close together, Zach and Rita were looking at the hill, too. Zach raised his hand to point something out to Rita, and then he caught sight of Nancy.

Slowly, he lowered his hand, watching Nancy the whole time. Not taking her eyes off him, either, Nancy started moving in their direction. She ignored the jostling crowds around her.

Suddenly, when she was about ten feet from them, Nancy stopped walking. Zach hadn't taken a single step, and now she saw why. In his hand, barely hidden by a jacket tossed over his arm, was the gun. He raised it and pointed it straight at her. In a flash, Nancy realized that he was waiting for the fireworks to start before firing it. It was a perfect cover. Between the exploding firecrackers and the screams of the crowd, no one would hear a single silenced shot that would leave her lying on the ground.

Chapter

Seventeen

As quickly as she could, Nancy glanced over her shoulder. The group of people in charge of the fireworks display had broken apart, and one man was checking his watch. Nancy realized that it was only a matter of seconds.

Looking back, she saw that Zach and Rita still hadn't moved. They were just waiting for the right moment.

Although there weren't crowds of people around her, there were people nearby. And Nancy knew that if she tried to protect herself, either she could lose Zach and Rita, or some innocent person could get hurt, or both. It wasn't worth the risk. She dropped her sandals and tossed her hair out of her eyes, but she stayed where she was.

The spectators became quieter. Shrieks of laughter died down to giggles, and loud conversations faded to soft murmurs. Nancy knew it was time for the fireworks—if she was going to do something, she had to do it then.

Before the first burst of a firecracker and the *whoosh* of a Roman candle shooting into the sky, Nancy ran and closed the gap between Zach and herself. And at the exact same moment that the club's most spectacular and biggest display got underway, Nancy leaped on him, both hands grabbing the arm that held the gun and forcing it straight up into the air.

The gun went off, its bullet shooting harmlessly into the sky, which was now filled with multicolored lights and bursting stars that glowed and then disappeared.

Nancy let go of Zach's arm with one hand, using it to dig her fingers into his throat. At the same time, she brought her knee up, giving him a sharp kick in the stomach.

Zach gasped and doubled over, and when he raised his head again, Nancy hit him on the jaw. Unconscious, he fell sideways onto the grass.

Breathing hard, Nancy looked for Rita, who was scrambling out of the area as fast as she could. Nancy stretched out her hand to grab the gun, when someone planted a foot on her wrist, pressing down hard and painfully.

Nancy looked up into the pale eyes of Max Fletcher.

"That was *very* exciting," Max said as he surreptitiously picked up and pocketed the gun. "But I'm afraid we've all had enough excitement for one night," he said to a couple of people who had glanced over to watch the antics on the ground.

Aiming the gun at her through his jacket pocket, Max said, "Come on, sweetie. Enough fooling around."

Slowly, Nancy got to her feet, keeping her eye on the gun.

"Oh, I'll use it all right," Max whispered into her ear. "Smile at anyone who looks at you, and walk nicely, or I will have to kill you."

Beside her, Nancy heard a low moan and realized that Zach was coming to. Rubbing his jaw, Zach got shakily to his feet and joined Max.

"Let's go now, shall we, sweetie?" Max said, smiling.

The fireworks were going strong; the sky was

lit up for miles, and the air reeked of gunpowder. Amazing, she thought, that just a couple of people even noticed what had happened. And they thought she and Zach were just goofing off.

As soon as they got close to the clubhouse, Nancy scanned the crowds for someone who knew her. If she could spot Detective Ryan, Ned, Bess, or George, she'd be all right. They'd *know* she was in trouble.

"Keep going," Max ordered, still in a whisper. "Around by the pool."

The crowd was thickest around the pool area, and Nancy hated the thought of getting into the middle of it. There wouldn't be room to try anything if she was packed in. But with a gun at her back, she didn't have much say in the matter.

As the three of them moved slowly through the crowd, a sudden shout went up. Nancy didn't pay much attention at first; it was probably just another reaction to the fireworks. Then she realized that the shout wasn't quite the same as the others she had been hearing. People weren't screaming in amazement over some fabulous pyrotechnic display. They were yelling because something completely unexpected had happened.

"I knew this was going to be a wild night,"

Nancy heard someone say. "But I still can't believe it. I mean, first the girl jumps into the diving pool with all her clothes on, and then the guy follows her, tie and all!"

A tie? Nancy thought. The only person who could possibly be wearing a tie to a Fourth of July party is Detective Ryan. And the only reason for him to be in the pool is that he's after Rita.

Glancing back, Nancy saw that Max and Zach hadn't paid any attention to the comment about the people in the pool. This was her chance.

Pretending that it was the only way to move through the crowd, Nancy began to make a path closer and closer to the diving pool. If I can get close enough, she thought, maybe Detective Ryan will see me.

When they reached the edge of the pool, Nancy looked down. In the middle of it, soaked to the skin, were Rita and Detective Ryan. Nancy was just about to call out when Zach spotted them. "Look," he said to Max. "It's Rita. She's been caught!"

"Too bad," Max commented. To Nancy, he whispered, "Keep moving. One word and I'll pull the trigger."

Nancy moved, but not the way Max had expected. She whirled around, reached out her

149

arms, and shoved. Losing his balance, Max crashed backward into Zach, and, like two dominoes, they fell into the water.

In the water, Rita was swimming as quickly as she could toward the edge. But Nancy planted herself in front of her. "You can get out, Rita," she said. "But that's about as far as you'll go." Then she called to Detective Ryan, "Look out, Detective, one of them has a gun!"

"Not anymore!" he shouted back. Holding the gun out of the water, the detective motioned for Zach and Max to swim to the side.

Dripping wet, the three thieves climbed out of the pool, followed by Detective Ryan. By this time, George, Ned, and Bess had joined Nancy, and the four friends watched as the detective put handcuffs on the culprits.

As he started to lead them away, Detective Ryan turned back to Nancy. "Pretty nice work, Ms. Drew," he said. Then he left.

Bess gasped, amazement written across her delicate features. "Is he serious?" she said. "You just caught the crooks for him single-handedly. If it hadn't been for you, they'd be out of town by now. And that's all the thanks you get?"

"Forget it," Nancy told her. "The detective's just not the grateful type, I guess. Anyway, the important thing is it's over. Finally, we can relax a little and watch the rest of the fireworks!"

"It's just fantastic!" Joanna said, plopping herself into a lounge chair beside Nancy. "I mean, you caught them, you found my necklace, and my parents don't get back until tomorrow!"

It was the fifth of July, and Nancy was back at the country club. When she had called Joanna that morning to tell her that the case had been solved, Joanna had insisted on meeting her at the club. "I've been away too long," Joanna had said. "I need some sun. Besides, I can't wait to tell everybody what happened."

After the last few days, the club was the last place Nancy wanted to be, but she had finally agreed.

"I didn't really find out where they kept the stuff they stole," Nancy said now. "Detective Ryan made them admit that Rita had stashed it in her apartment."

"Oh, don't be so modest," Joanna said. "If it hadn't been for you, I'd be in big trouble. But now? As I said, my parents will be slightly mad, but once they know the necklace is back, they'll be calm about it all."

"Do you mind if I give you some advice?" Nancy asked.

"No, go ahead."

"Don't talk so much," Nancy suggested.

Joanna looked insulted.

"I mean, don't talk so much about the things you have," Nancy said quickly. "Especially the expensive things. And don't let the whole world know when your house will be empty. You never know who might be listening."

"Believe me, I'm going to keep my mouth shut from now on," Joanna said. Then, as she saw the lifeguard coming out of the clubhouse, she cried, "Mike! Guess what? Nancy found my necklace! It's a good thing I never told Max or Zach or Rita about that safe in the dining room, isn't it? That's where my parents keep cash, and I'm not talking about small bills, either!"

Shaking her head, Nancy decided to leave. Joanna would never change, but if she was lucky, maybe she'd never run into another Zach or Rita.

As Nancy walked toward her car, she almost bumped into Detective Ryan. He was wearing a striped tie, but otherwise he looked the same—grimly serious.

"Hi," Nancy said. "How did everything go after I left last night?"

"By the book," the detective said. "I just

came to tell Ms. Tate that her necklace will have to be used as evidence, so she won't get it back as soon as she thought."

"Uh-oh," Nancy said. "She's not going to be very happy about that."

Detective Ryan looked annoyed. "What does she expect?" he asked. "Does she think everything that happened was just a bad dream?"

"Something like that," Nancy said. "But don't worry. Even if she doesn't like it, she'll cooperate."

"Good." The detective started to walk away, and then he stopped. "By the way," he said, "I don't know if I told you, but you did a good job."

"You told me," Nancy said. "You said, 'pretty nice work.'" She laughed. "I expected you to say 'pretty nice work, for an *amateur.*'"

To her surprise, Detective Ryan shook his head, chuckling the way he had in the locker room the night before.

"What's so funny this time?" Nancy asked.

"Same thing," he said. "I might as well admit it. I was laughing at myself because I couldn't believe how stupid I'd been not to listen to you."

"I've got an idea," Nancy said with a grin.

"Why don't we try to work together from now on? We might solve more cases. And if it doesn't work out, well, we can always break the truce and start arguing again. Deal, Detective Ryan?"

He grinned back. "Deal, Detective Drew."

Nancy's next case:

An urgent phone call from old friend Susan Victors brings Nancy to a California campus —and a sorority under a cloud. Rina Charles hinted that something rotten was going on. Now she's dead. Was it a scuba accident, as most of the girls believe—or was it murder?

There's no end of suspects. Nancy finds herself investigating a whole houseful of beautiful, intelligent, and charming college girls—except that one of them has a deadly secret.

Will Nancy pierce that secret? Find out in *SISTERS IN CRIME*, Case #19 in The Nancy Drew Files™.